The Ice Gorilla

Written by
Michael Esola

Story by
Wesley Jones

Mantra Press

The Ice Gorilla

ISBN: 978-0-578-09050-4
eBook ISBN: 978-1-618-42146-3

Published by Mantra Press
First Edition

Printed in the United States of America

10 9 8 7 6 5 4 3 2 1

Dedication

From Michael
To all those willing to pay the price to follow their dreams.

From Wesley
This book is dedicated to my parents, who made sure that I was instilled with a strong foundation of core values, and to my loving wife, who tolerates me on those long nights of writing.

Prologue

Despite the technological and informational age in which we live, Earth still remains the grandmaster of mystery and intrigue.

Drop any individual into one of the many rainforest ecosystems of the world, and there is a good chance, if they are brave enough to pick up one of the insect inhabitants, that it will be a brand new species to science. This represents our current understanding of the world. The oceans and rainforests of the world might as well be alien landscapes in regard to the amount of secrets waiting to be unearthed and discovered.

The world is an enigmatic and vast place, with many secret and hidden areas which lie far away from the eye of humans and civilization. There remain many valleys tucked in and around mountain ranges that are isolated from most everyone. Places such as the Amazon are treasure troves of biological diversity in terms of flora and fauna.

It's quite possible that one day someone will venture deep into a rainforest ecosystem like the Amazon, and discover a python so large it dwarfs anything comprehensible by today's standards. The same goes for the Earth's oceans, in that there are many unexplored rifts and trenches. Maybe one day someone will discover that the extinct prehistoric shark Megalodon still patrols the Earth's waters.

The greatest predator on earth is neither man nor beast. It is time, for it is always hunting us, and it will never rest or sleep. It will continue to hunt us until our last day.

---Dr. Stephen Chee

The Ice Gorilla

Chapter One

The snow continued to fall heavily while the gray clouds provided the storm with strength. In the distance the snow covered mountains sat, ancient, timeless, and looming over the massive ice shelf directly in front of them.

The wind whipped back and forth rapidly, as the single beat up, black snowmobile raced across snow covered terrain, leaving two long and solitary lines every foot that it traversed. In pursuit were two red snowmobiles, and they were gaining ground quickly, as they thundered across the open terrain. The two drivers continued onward, hell-bent on reaching the black snowmobile.

A loud boom reverberated across the ice field as the black snowmobile crashed down on the other side of an open crevasse, the driver just narrowly missing a fatal encounter with the deep and dark depths below. The driver looked back quickly to see how far behind the pursuers were. They were close on his tail, closing the gap with each second.

In an effort to gain on the speedy black snowmobile, one of the red snowmobile drivers took a calculated risk and sped up as they approached the open crevasse. Miscalculating the jump, the driver crashed into the side of the crevasse. The impact left him and his snowmobile engulfed in flames, as he fell back plummeting to his death.

Screams of agony could be heard as the other trailing red snowmobile flew over the crevasse, smashing down on the other side.

The driver of the black snowmobile could see that the red one was gaining on him. In an act to divert him, the black snowmobile veered sharply to the right, catching the red snowmobile slightly off guard.

The second driver increased his speed, finally catching up to and ramming the black snowmobile.

To gain the upper hand outright, the red snowmobile rammed the black snowmobile once more, the impact causing little more than an annoyance to the black one as it continued on at a breakneck pace.

The red snowmobile suddenly surged ahead and rammed into the side of the black one, once, twice, the impact causing the driver to hit the snow, rolling head over heels. His snowmobile exploded as it crashed into one of the open crevasses.

The driver, dazed and confused, lay there for a fleeting moment, not quite certain what had just happened.

The red snowmobile circled the driver and pulled up as the driver of the fallen snowmobile, now fully coming to his senses, edged backwards.

The man on the ice continued to pull himself backwards and quickly looked over his shoulder, but there was nowhere to run or hide. He continued to pull himself backwards as the first shot was fired by the man standing.

The shot hit the driver square in the chest, and slowly his body fell, lifeless.

The attacker approached the man on the ice, bent down, and retrieved from the man's coat, a bloodied, white cloth, wrapped around a large object.

He quickly stuffed it into his jacket, took a few steps from the man and fired two more shots into the lifeless body.

He quickly zoomed away on his snowmobile and disappeared into the white landscape.

Chapter Two

Will Freeman, mid-thirties, stood in front of one of the many exhibits, holding a sandwich in one hand. He was slender with wavy brown hair. He was plainly dressed, befitting a college professor.

He had been standing in front of the elaborate polar bear exhibit for quite some time. The exhibit showcased the world's largest land carnivore, the massive polar bear. It described in great detail the loss of habitat and the fact that many of these animals drown while swimming land to land, a direct result of the melting of their environment.

Will checked his wrist watch. "Where the hell is he?"

He noticed that he wasn't alone as a mother and her child stood next to him, looking at the exhibit. The young child pulled at her mother's arms and surprised everyone by blurting out, "Big monster!"

Will smiled. He looked down at the girl who was now pointing at the large polar bear in astonishment. For a brief moment, he marveled at the wide-eyed innocence of the child, the belief that anything and everything was indeed possible in life. He envied the child in a way, wishing that he could re-live his own childhood, as there were so many things he didn't get to experience growing up. Always having his head buried in a book, keeping his eye on the goal, put an end to his child-hood at a very young age.

Bending to the level of the child he smiled and said, "that's a polar bear. Can you say polar bear?"

"Po bear," she muttered.

"Rarrr," motioning his hand toward the girl in the form of a claw.

She instantly started to cry, and turned away toward her mother. She hastily grabbed the child by the hand, giving Will a nasty look as they quickly walked away.

Will raised his hand in apology, "sorry."

He stood there for a few seconds, watching both turn and walk down the corridor toward another display.

What the hell went wrong? No wonder I don't have kids, he thought to himself.

"They were out of decaf," Peter said, startling Will half to death.

"Out of it or too cheap to buy me a cup," Will fired back.

"Both," Peter said.

Peter Miles stood there in all his glory with his hands at his hips. Like a statue he posed, standing for all to see as if he was one of the exhibits. He was casually dressed. His stylish haircut and neck-chain also accentuated his statuesque pose. He looked, by all accounts, the epitome of success.

The men slowly strolled past several exhibits, pausing only for a few seconds to observe, and then moved on. Time was always money with Peter.

"How are book sales?" Will asked, breaking the air of silence.

Peter nodded his head slightly, "going into its second print and I'm buying a new Lexus next month."

"Must be nice," Will replied.

Peter stopped, "I didn't become a best-selling author overnight you know. I worked my tail off, ate Raman soup after Raman soup, and got rejected by publishers more than is good for the human soul. You can do it too. You just need to get out of this rut."

Will shook his head and looked down at the ground. "Maybe one day."

Peter grabbed him by the shoulders, startling him. "No, today, Will. You can do this shit today. Too many people in life say that they'll do something tomorrow. You know what that's called?"

"Procrastinating," Will replied.

Peter shook his head. "No, my friend. It's called, afraid to grab the bull by the horns."

They passed several more exhibits before Will paused for a moment in front of a large gorilla exhibit showcasing the true size and strength of the Silverback gorilla.

Peter paid no attention to the exhibit as he leaned against the rail, people-watching or "Peter watching" as he liked to call it as the hordes passed by them.

Will looked down at the sign. "You know that sign says, 'No leaning on the rail'."

Peter shook his head once again. "Man, there must be something strange in that place you call home," pointing to his head and then to Will's head. "Something funny in the water, I tell ya. Tell me that you're going to Big Al's tonight?"

"I think I'll pass," Will replied, walking toward the sign for the gorilla exhibit.

"How about hiking this weekend?"

Will shook his head. "No thanks."

Peter appeared slightly agitated. "Biking?"

Peter followed, as Will headed for the nearest seat by the great hall of exhibits.

"You know, Will," Peter said, sitting down next to his friend, "it's time to move on. Kari died over a year ago. You have to get out there. Experience the world for a change. You're caught in the ivory tower and need to get out before it's too late."

Will somewhat taken aback by the harshness of the statement, stared straight ahead. "I can't. Not yet. And I'm not stuck in the ivory tower, I'm just busy working in it."

Peter sighed. "Either way, your body's still in it, and the rest of the world is going on outside as you rot away inside. I'm tired of always hearing, maybe tomorrow, from you. Grab that metaphorical bull by the horns."

A young woman walked by, shaking her head, obviously having overheard their conversation.

"You see?" Peter said, pointing to her, and making sure to speak loudly and clearly, "women like guys who grab life by the horns."

She turned and gave Peter a sarcastic look, but she cracked a smile for Will.

Peter took a much needed sip of his coffee, which was getting colder by the minute. "It's time to break free! Now is your chance, and you can start by going to Big Al's tonight."

Peter took a quick glance at his watch. "I'm late for a meeting with the Chancellor. Think about what I said."

"I have a two o'clock lecture back on campus," Will replied, standing up hastily.

Peter swatted Will on the back as he bolted for the exit. "Stop playing it safe! See you at Big Al's."

Will returned to the main part of the museum and approached the large woolly mammoth exhibit in the center of the room. He looked up at the great beast from many eons ago. Its massive body, covered in fur, gave it a larger-than-life appearance. Will let his mind roam for a minute, thinking back to the days of his childhood when he would close his eyes, and imagine what it would have been like to be around during the time of the dinosaurs.

He gripped the hand railing and squeezed it tightly as he envisioned the past, imagining primitive man trying to take down such an animal with his handmade weapons.

Would have been quite a sight, would have been quite a sight indeed, he thought to himself.

Chapter Three

The bright sun beamed down on the campus full of students. Some were reading on the grass, others socializing, some partaking in football or frisbee.

Will quickly walked down a brick pathway lined with weeds. Slung over his shoulder was a brown briefcase that had seen better days, a zoology book in his left hand. He had been to a few personal development seminars over the years, and they had always stressed carrying objects in one's left hand, so as to leave the right one free with which to shake a person's hand. He was trying hard to put what he learned into practice.

He made his way out into the open courtyard which was surrounded by old brick buildings. It was a very quaint spot, serving as a place for students to gather, for concerts, or for protests. It was the week before finals and was rather empty.

Two students tossed a red frisbee back-and-forth, catching Will's attention. One of the students waved, and Will waved back.

"Doctor Freeman," a voice from behind called.

Will turned and saw Dean Adams approaching.

"Dean," he said, somewhat surprised.

She was a short woman, in her mid-fifties, and she wore a gray suit with a BlackBerry attached to her hip.

She quickly approached Will and they walked together toward the Arts and Sciences Building.

"Nice work on that article about the South Pole," she said.

Will cracked a small smile. "Thank you, Dean."

"Ever been?"

"Can't say that I have," Will replied, shaking his head.

Without warning, Dean Adams stopped abruptly and grabbed Will's arm. The act caused Will's heart to sink, knowing, that all of a sudden, the situation had changed from a friendly encounter to a more serious one.

"I know our schedules are hectic, but we need to talk," Dean Adams said in a serious tone.

Will came to a full and complete stop and now stood facing Dean Adams head on. Her hands were now at her hips.

For a brief moment, Will marveled at Dean Adams's beauty. Though she was in her fifties, time had treated her well. Dean Adams's voice broke into his thoughts.

"The university is cutting back the zoology and other selected programs," she said.

At that exact moment Will felt as if all life had escaped his body, like everything he had ever owned and worked for had been violently pulled out from under him.

She grabbed Will's elbow as he appeared very shocked and unsteady.

"Your position is being eliminated after the semester, and right now there's no other position I can offer."

Will stood in utter shock, not knowing quite what to say or how to react. Suddenly, Dean Adams's BlackBerry rang.

She quickly grabbed it and glanced down at the screen. "I have to take this. I'm so sorry, Will."

Quickly walking away she proceeded to answer the call. "This is Dean Adams."

Will followed the Dean with his eyes. He was unsure from what his eyes were seeing and what his brain was thinking, just what was real.

Chapter Four

Will stood at the front of the classroom, listening to his students. He peered absent mindedly across the large lecture hall of students.

"Did you hear my theory Doctor Freeman?" asked a student.

Will continued to look across the lecture hall as if he was alone in the room.

"Doctor Freeman?"

"I'm sorry, Cindy" Will finally responded. "A lot on the mind right now, but you make a great point. My concern is that does anyone really care anymore?"

Will turned his back on the room full of confused students thinking how his life had diminished within hours.

He turned back to face the students. "Final exam next week, open book. That's all I have for today."

Many students looked shocked as they began to exit the room. The concept of open book exams were a foreign language in Will's lesson plan. A group of concerned students approached Will as he slowly packed up his beat up brief case.

"Open book test?" asked one confused student.

"You guys deserve it. You worked hard all semester."

"Not that we're complaining, but 'Professor.Com' says you never have given an open book test."

Will gave the group an empty look. "Take it while you can."

As the group exited the room Will placed his hands on the table and looked across the lecture hall. *Take it while you can, nobody will even know what a Zoologist will be,* he thought to himself.

He walked around the rustic desk and walked up the steps taking in the sight and smell of the environment. He walked down one of the aisles and sat in a chair for a moment to gain a student's perspective. On the white board were notes from his class lecture on the future of global warming and its impact on all life forms.

After a few moments of quiet thoughts he got up from his chair and returned to the front of the lecture hall. He grabbed his old briefcase, saluted the whiteboard, as if to dismiss it as nonsense, and tossed his briefcase into the wastebasket next to the desk.

Will quietly exited the deserted lecture hall, leaving only a few theories written on the whiteboard and his old briefcase in the wastebasket.

Chapter Five

A black, shiny Mercedes pulled into the parking lot of Big Al's Bar with Peter behind the wheel. He drove to the end of the lot and parked in an isolated spot. This, hopefully, would guarantee that no nicks or dents would be inflicted on his precious car by careless patrons.

With his phone to his ear, he parked the car with one hand while still managing to carry on his conversation. Peter had never been one to follow the law, and talking on the phone while driving was one that he routinely broke.

"Love you, too. Don't wait up."

Peter shut his phone off and set it down on the passenger seat. He took one more look at it and decided to put it in the glove box. He spent the entire day on the phone, and the last thing he wanted was an email, text, or phone call at this point.

He took one last look in the mirror and ran his hand through his hair. A quick dash of cologne and he was ready to go.

"Damn, you look good," he said to himself, pointing to his reflection in the mirror.

Walking through the parking lot, Peter had a confident and sexy stride about him, the kind that made him very attractive to women and the envy of men. He quite often referred to himself as the modern day Steve McQueen, though these comparisons were always done in private.

As he swung the heavy door open, he was greeted by a solid wall of sound, chatter, and good old-fashioned fun as patrons played darts and shot pool. Clouds of smoke rose to fill the old rustic saloon. It was very much the college scene that one would imagine.

The place was packed. Every barstool and booth was filled with students. Music played in the background, courtesy of an old-time jukebox in the corner.

Zac, a muscular man, in his thirties, with a clean-shaven head, chomped down on a saucy buffalo wing around four students in their twenties. He tossed the bone into a metal bucket full of other discarded bones that he had finished off. Clink! He proceeded to quickly chug down a full mug of beer and slammed the empty mug down on the table.

Chug! Chug! Chug!

"That's how you do it, boys and girls," he said while belching half way through.

The students looked at Zac, one of the more exciting, personable, and charismatic professors on campus, and laughed. He was never too busy to have buffalo wings or toss back a few beers with his students. He was quite commonly referred to as the coolest professor on campus, a label that made him a favorite amongst the students but led to scorn and irritation with the faculty.

"Now," Zac said as he wiped his mouth, "I expect a full page report on my desk tomorrow that includes beer temperature, current, and changes in salinity."

Zac looked around and grabbed a mug of beer from the table and raised it in the air. "Here's to climatology and the non-existent future of our program! May the university flood away when this global warming shit hits."

The group clinked mugs and chugged down their beers.

"After my unemployment runs out, I'm gonna be a brew master! Sam Adams ain't got shit on me," Zac proudly proclaimed.

"I'll drink to that," a student shouted out.

Zac took another drink from the pitcher of beer at the table. Peter appeared and approached the group of students.

"Seen Will?"

"Fifth beer and haven't seen him," Zac replied, causing a wry laugh from the group.

Peter just shook his head. His attention was diverted by the female bartender who had smiled several times at him already.

"Now, whose ass can I kick at darts," Zac proclaimed at the top of his lungs, slamming the pitcher down on the table.

Chapter Six

The phone rang in Will's dimly lit living room. The shades were drawn, giving the room a dark and gloomy feel.

Despite the dreary appearance, everything sat meticulously organized and clean. Next to the ringing phone was a wedding photo of Will and his late wife Kari.

On his mahogany desk was a wedding photo of Will, Peter, and Zac, all dressed in their stunning tuxedos.

Academic achievement awards and his college degrees, including his doctoral degree hung in perfect alignment on the wall. The telephone continued to ring.

Will sat, slumped on the couch facing the blank television screen, as tears streamed down his face. His eyes were red, face blotchy, symbolizing both the pain and frustration he was suffering.

His body was pretty much limp, as if all life had somehow dissipated from his human form. In front of him on the coffee table stood a half-full bottle of vodka and an empty shot glass.

He tried to straighten himself up as he slowly sat up on the couch, but continued to stare aimlessly at the blank television screen.

Will held a paper up to the light. It read "Foreclosure Notice" in bright red at the top.

A knock at the front door broke the air of silence. The knocking continued as Will continued to sit there, in a trancelike state.

Knock! Knock! Knock!

Peter stood outside the front door, which was open with the rod-iron screen door closed. He walked to a window on the side of the house and could see Will sitting on the couch. Peter was confused.

"Will," he shouted, banging on the window. "Will!"

Will didn't budge an inch nor did he even make a motion that he heard Peter outside.

Peter stood there for a second. "Shit!" He made his way back a few feet, lowered his shoulder, and in one fell swoop move, rammed through the screen door into Will's house.

Peter ran through the foyer and into the living room, only to see Will still sitting with a blank expression on his face.

"Will," Peter said, standing to the side of his good friend.

He continued to stare at the blank television screen. Peter glanced at the screen and then back at his friend.

"Hey, man, you okay?" Peter said as he moved in closer to Will's trembling body.

He noticed a .32 handgun on the coffee table.

"It's okay, Will. I'm just gonna take this from you."

Peter slowly reached for and picked up the .32 handgun and set it on the desk, several feet from Will.

Will turned from the screen and slowly turned to Peter with a agonized expression.

"It wasn't over a year ago. It was one year tonight."

Flashback

A flashlight illuminated a bedroom, as rummaging through a desk drawer occurred. Objects from the desk were being dumped onto the floor.

The flashlight illumination moved out into the hallway and into the living room. Rifling through another desk drawer could be heard.

The front door squeaked open and shut. The foyer lights turned on. Kari entered the room, wearing a black skirt, her blonde hair flowing behind her.

She was instantly set upon by the intruder, dressed in black clothing, his face covered with a black ski mask. Scared half to death, she tried to reach for the telephone on the end table.

The intruder and Kari struggled. She kicked and clawed at the intruder, causing the strong assailant to drop the flashlight.

Kari, desperate in her attempt to get the intruder off her, grabbed a letter opener off the top of the mahogany desk and attempted to stab the attacker. Swinging several times she missed.

The intruder knocked the letter opener out of Kari's hand and to the floor, pushing her to the floor as well.

She struggled under the weight of the assailant.

Stab. Stab. Stab.

Chapter Seven

"It should have been me," Will muttered, holding his head in his hands, tears streaming down his face.

Peter moved in, and sat next to him. "You can't keep doing this to yourself. You have no choice but to move on, or you'll wither away in this place."

Will looked up as tears ran down his face. "Why the hell not? They never even found the bastard!"

Peter stood up from where he sat, "it's like I said earlier, you have to live your life. It's time to move on. We're all sad for Kari, but what the hell can any of us do about it. It's time for you to move on to the next chapter of your life."

Will sat with his arms folded and slouched down in the couch. "I can't go on living."

"Yes, you can," Peter said, as he took hold of the vodka bottle and the handgun. "But not like this."

Peter got up from the couch and placed the vodka on the desk in the corner. He smiled to himself, checking the barrel of the .32 handgun. "You know these don't work without bullets."

Will gave him a blank stare.

Peter grabbed a blanket from the couch. "Man, sometimes you crack me up."

"You hear about work?" Will asked.

"I know. Sorry, man."

"What?" Will remarked in disbelief. "You didn't get let go?"

Peter sat and reclined back in a chair with his arms behind his head. "Luck of the Irish, I suppose. Guess they had mercy on me. After this book, I'm trying to work it so I don't have to go back to teaching."

Will shook his head in disbelief, not quite taking in what he was hearing. Peter threw the blanket on the recliner next to the couch.

"What are you doing?" Will asked.

"You think I'm gonna let my good friend be alone in his misery. I can't let you have all the fun. I'm staying the night to make sure you see daylight."

Peter glanced at the blank television screen and then back toward Will. He grabbed the remote control from the coffee table. "Enough of this blank screen crap. This silence is deafening."

He turned the television on and went straight to The Ski Channel, his favorite.

Chapter Eight

The sun beamed down upon Peter and Will, as they strode toward Peter's black Mercedes parked in the driveway. A goodnight's sleep had done both of them wonders. Will had a certain pep in his step, as he picked up his morning paper and tossed it back toward his porch.

Birds chirped, and several dogs from the neighborhood barked. Two neighbors jogged past on their morning run.

Peter looked back toward the front door. "Sorry about the screen door."

"Needed a new one anyway," Will said. "Nothing that Lowe's or Home Depot can't solve."

Peter's black, shiny car was flawless. It radiated wealth and high social class. He wiped the car with a cloth to remove a small smudge.

"Go talk to the chancellor," Peter said as he closed the door. "See what he has to say."

The engine started and he slowly backed down the driveway. Peter pointed at Will and shouted, "new beginnings!"

The black Mercedes peeled out the minute it hit the street, leaving black tire marks for quite some distance.

"Slow down," Will's neighbor shouted. "Asshole!"

She had been watching the entire time. Though she was in her eighties, she was still very spry and feisty.

"Don't worry about him, Mrs. Phelps. He's harmless," Will said, heading back toward his front door.

"Losers," she muttered, continuing to water her geraniums.

Chapter Nine

The tiny, cramped office was taken up by a desk, chair, and small cluttered shelves. The window to the outside world was small, roughly 11" by 16" in size. Stacks of paper covered the floor, shelves, and desk, all in neat piles, giving off the hint that there was some method to this madness.

The trash can overflowed with crumpled paper. Across from the desk was a door leading into another room.

Sitting behind the desk was Jonathon, in his early twenties with gelled brown hair. He wore a gray suit and red tie.

Jonathon was Chancellor Stephen Chee's personal assistant, but to everyone around campus he was more commonly referred to as his personal gofer. He was despised by many for his close relationship with the chancellor. Many had spotted shady practices in the way of expensive gifts from Chee to Jonathon, but no one dared report it, for fear of the consequences.

He was speaking on his Blue Tooth when Will walked into the tiny room.

"I'm not sure if I have the right place," Will said, examining his surroundings.

"Hurry it up," Jonathan said while typing away on his laptop at a fast speed.

Will took a half step forward and stated, "I have a two o 'clock with the Chancellor."

"A two o 'clock what?" Jonathon fired back, refusing to make eye contact with Will.

Taken aback, Will replied, "A two o 'clock meeting…with the chancellor." *What the hell's this guy's problem?* He thought to himself.

Jonathon didn't look up at him. "Be more specific. The Chancellor values time greater than anyone at this institution. Take a seat."

Baffled, Will looked around the office. There was barely enough room for one person, let alone two adults.

"That's okay, I'll just stand."

He then noticed the sign that hung directly above the door that led to the other room. It promptly read, "THE GREATEST PREDATOR ON EARTH IS NEITHER MAN NOR BEAST. IT IS TIME, FOR IT IS ALWAYS HUNTING US, AND IT WILL NEVER REST OR SLEEP. IT WILL CONTINUE TO HUNT US UNTIL OUR LAST DAY."

Will took a deep breath. *Psycho*, he thought to himself.

Suddenly Zac came bobbing through the door, wearing khaki shorts, sunglasses, a polo shirt, and sandals. "Is this the unemployment line?"

Will looked over, slightly surprised. "What are you doing here?"

"Same as you, looking for work."

In a very rude manner, Jonathon examined Zac starting at his feet and slowly working his way up. "May I help you?"

"You sure can."

"Do you have an appointment?" Jonathon asked, not looking up, but beginning to type.

Zac stepped forward slightly. "You made it. Two P.M... Zac."

"Very well," Jonathon said, while finally looking up from the keyboard. "The Chancellor will see both of you in a moment. Please have a seat."

"Where?" Zac confusingly asked. "In your chair?"

Jonathon gave Zac another snide look as Zac leaned on the wall next to Will.

"What a jack off?" he whispered to Will.

"What's this about?" Will whispered back.

"You tell me. Got a breath mint?"

Will shook his head no.

The ringing telephone on Jonathon's desk broke the uncomfortable silence. He tapped his Blue Tooth. "Very well, sir. I'll send them right in."

Jonathon stood up from his desk and walked the men over to the closed door. "The Chancellor will now see both of you."

Chapter Ten

Will and Zac found the Chancellor's office to be absolutely stunning. A large bay window overlooked a massive aspen tree. A red velvet pool table sat in front of a real log-burning fireplace with a cherry-finish mantel. High above was a crystal adorned chandelier in the very center of the room. It capped off the magnificent and elegant setting.

Chancellor Stephen Chee sat at his beautiful mahogany desk as the men approached. He was in his fifties, Asian, short in stature, but his appearance was stunning. He appeared slick and extraordinary, his black suit flawless. One could see his or her own reflection in his black shoes.

"Greetings, gentlemen," he said as he rose to his feet to greet them. His English was always nothing short of superb and proper.

"Now I know why I'm losin' my job," Zac remarked as he scanned the surroundings.

Will nudged him with his elbow.

"Let me get straight to the point, gentlemen."

Chee motioned to the red velvet chairs in front of the large desk. "Please have a seat."

Chee waited for the two to be seated before seating himself at his desk. "I know about your current work situation, and it is unfortunate."

"No shit," Zac blurted out.

Chee looked at Zac in silence.

"As I was to say," he said. "I have a proposition for both of you."

Chee tapped a button on his keyboard. A large screen came down on the wall from the ceiling behind him, and the lights in the room began to dim.

The room took on a very theater-like feel, as if the latest Hollywood blockbuster feature film was about to be shown.

The screen illuminated a majestic image of an expansive ice shelf. The giant sheet of ice next to frigid blue waters caused both Will and Zac to sit forward in their chairs. The solid mass of ice was smooth, running all the way down into the dark, icy blue water below.

"The Ward Hunt Ice Shelf," Chee said, pointing from the side of the screen.

Will looked on, intrigued.

"As I was saying, the Ward Hunt Ice Shelf is in the Canadian Arctic. It is about one hundred fifty square miles in size. It is rapidly becoming in danger of breaking off, and the climate is changing. It is a formidable journey for anyone who dares to visit, but a profitable one for the right reasons."

"Global warming, huh," Zac remarked.

The lights came back on and the screen moved back up into the ceiling. Will was instantly brought back to the real world and his, and Zac's current plight.

Chee moved closer to them, leaning over the desk. "Gentlemen, I did not bring you here to have a philosophical debate on global warming. I operate on a very simple philosophy. Global warming is indeed happening, but whether or not we are the culprits, that is entirely too difficult to deduce and, therefore, an utter waste of my time."

"Man," Zac said, "for a second there I thought you might be some kind of travel agent. You aren't a travel agent, are you?" he asked Chee in a joking manner. "Between the two of us, I'd prefer somewhere a little warmer."

Chee looked at him in a serious manner without responding to the question.

"Again gentlemen," he said, "I am forming a team to go up there, and, by there, I mean The Ward Hunt Ice Shelf. The plane leaves tomorrow. I want the two of you on that plane."

He leaned over the desk and watched Will and Zac with anticipation.

Will shook his head slightly. "Why us? Why now? And I'm not certain I understand what this is about."

"Sometimes, Mr. Freeman, it is best to accept offers without questions."

"You're proposing we head out into the middle of nowhere. I think it's very wise to ask questions."

"Very well Mr. Freeman. I have arranged for T.A.'s to administer your final exams, and from my understanding neither of you have anything to lose."

Zac sat up and smirked. "Except maybe some toes and part of a nose. Frostbite out there can be a bitch."

"Maybe on an ill-prepared expedition, but I can assure you, this is not an ill-prepared expedition," Chee said as he strolled to the far side of the desk. "We have spared no expense."

Will still remained confused. "But why us? It's a big university and an even bigger universe for that matter."

Chee strode confidently to the other corner of his desk and inserted a key into the top-left desk drawer.

Will was amazed to see such a large and ornate key. It was a throwback to the keys of yesteryear, a big bulky object that would have taken up an entire pocket.

Chee paused for a moment and then turned the key. They could hear the key turning inside the lock.

Slowly, Chee opened the desk drawer, and pulled out a large wooden box that appeared, upon first glance, to be too big for the drawer. It was ornate and made of the finest Brazilian wood. He placed the box on the desk.

Chee looked up, scrutinizing them, with a serious but non-threatening look. "What I am about to show you will change your lives and enlighten you as to why you will get on that plane tomorrow."

Will continued to stare at the box, as if almost refusing to look at Chee. The silence held as no one spoke a word.

Chee then pulled out another key, this time much smaller in size than the previous one. Slowly and carefully he inserted it into the wooden box.

He turned the key, pausing for a moment before he finally opened the box. Carefully and meticulously he pulled out a giant black claw and placed it on the desk before the men.

For a few seconds not a word was uttered. The claw had a nice dark black sheen to it and was slightly over one foot in length, massive by any account. It appeared as if it might have been from some type of predatory dinosaur, a scary reminder of the prehistoric animals that once existed.

Will knew better however than to expect it might be from a dinosaur such as T-Rex or Spinosaurus.

"What the hell's that?" Zac all of the sudden blurted out, breaking the silence.

At Zac's words, he and Will slid their chairs closer to what was being presented before their very eyes.

"Gentlemen," Chee said. "This was obtained from the Ward Hunt Ice Shelf not too long ago in isolated terrain. I trust you two have never seen anything the likes of it before?"

Will shook his head, gazing down at the giant claw. "It looks like it could be from some type of primate, but it's obviously far too large."

"It remains a conundrum, Mr. Freeman."

"Ca what?" Zac asked.

Chee didn't respond, but stared at Zac for a moment. "As I was saying, this is something brand new to science, the likes of which the world has never seen."

Chee stood and walked to the magnificent bookshelf display that lined the wall to the right of his desk. He turned, with his hands behind his back, and addressed both men. "I want the rest of it. All of it. It is worth a substantial amount to the right client."

Chee placed the claw back in the box.

"So, you're asking us to go hunt for Big Foot?" Zac said.

Chee smiled. "What I am asking is for you to use your fields of expertise to help me with this expedition. Think of it as a business proposition with a heavy science component. You know this kind of species, or close to it," he said to Will. "And you, know the climate," Chee said to Zac.

Will shook his head. "Hard to say what I know. We're dealing with a claw here, nothing more."

"Yes, we are dealing with a claw, Mr. Freeman," Chee replied, "but I need both of you to open your eyes to the possibilities. This is something amazing. The chance of a lifetime, to make a discovery like this, to rewrite the history books, to make history instead of reading about it. I am offering both of you, the chance at fame and fortune."

Neither said a word in reply to him.

Chee took a deep breath and stared up at the ceiling. "I knew that bringing you here this afternoon would indeed be difficult, but before I get into the financial aspect at stake here, let me make a few other points."

"Are we about done here?" Zac asked, moving about in his chair, fighting restless leg syndrome. "The batting cages are calling my name."

Once again Chee didn't respond but stared at him for a moment and shook his head. "You are an interesting life form, but a valuable one."

"That's what I've been told," Zac replied.

"I will keep it short, gentlemen," he said. "What this expedition means for both of you, is the chance to validate your careers."

Chee glared in Zac's direction. "With this expedition you can prove that global warming is becoming an issue of extreme serious concern."

Chee then looked Will directly in the eyes, "And you can prove your kind is needed in academia."

"The university has already made its decision," Will replied.

"Yes," Chee said. "However, a successful expedition can help my argument with the state, to continue funding your respective programs."

"And your wallet," Zac blurted out.

Will stood up and proceeded toward the door, alone.

"$500,000 for each of you," the words gripping Will, as he was about to step through the doorway.

Will paused for a moment and looked back at Zac who had an excited and eager look on his face.

"Come on, Will, don't be stupid," Zac said. "It's not just the money. Like Peter says, new beginnings. This is your chance. Don't die with regrets."

Will lowered his head for a moment, turned away from both men, and reached into his wallet. He pulled out a picture of his late wife, Kari, and gazed at it for a moment.

"New beginnings," he quietly whispered to himself. "New beginnings."

He turned and faced Chee, who was still looking at him with the stare of a cold-hearted emotionless reptile. "Deal."

Chee cracked a slight smile. "Wise choice, Mr. Freeman. Wise choice indeed."

"I have one condition," Will said.

Zac, still astonished that Will had accepted the offer, looked over again at his good friend.

"That we get to conduct the research needed to help save and promote our programs."

"Very well," Chee replied. "We leave tomorrow at eighteen hundred hours."

The men exited the splendid office, as Chee sat back down at his desk, the epitome of success, at the helm of his magnificently crafted enterprise. He picked up the phone in a hasty manner. "Come in now."

Jonathon entered the office almost as quickly as Chee hung up the phone.

"Yes, sir."

"Did you make all the necessary arrangements?"

Jonathon nodded. "Why do we need them, sir? The last group was hunters, and they failed. These two aren't even close to the type of people that we need."

"My point indeed, Mr. Madson."

"Sir?"

"My father taught me to never make the same mistake twice. The first group was hunters, and they failed miserably. This time around we will not make the same mistake."

Jonathon smiled slightly.

Chee walked over to the enormous bay window with his hands behind his back, glaring out the large window. He dismissed Jonathan "that is all." Jonathon quickly exited the room.

Chapter Eleven

The aircraft hangar began to brighten, as daylight poured in from the many cracks in the surface of the ceiling of the old and dilapidated building. A mid-sized cargo plane with its back ramp open stood waiting. The plane had seen better days. The writing on the side of it was barely discernible. The color had faded into no distinguishable hue.

In front of the long ramp that led in to the plane were parked, three black snowmobiles. The snowmobiles appeared to be brand new, fresh out-of-the-box.

Down the back ramp came Dobs, in his forties, with long black hair and two gold, front teeth. Following close behind, was Brooks, also in his forties. The men were completely covered in sweat, their overalls filthy with grease.

"And don't forget to charge the satellite phones," Peter shouted from the middle of the hangar.

Dobs nodded his head and muttered to himself, "yeah, yeah, yeah."

"Hey!" Brooks shouted, "help me get that climbing gear pushed in. That shit's heavy."

Dobs gave him a wry look. "What the hell do I look like?"

Brooks laughed. "Like shit. Now gimme a hand."

The two made their way around the back of the plane and went out of view up the ramp.

An awkward screeching sound could be heard from somewhere close by as Will and Zac walked in with suitcases in hand. Will led the way with Zac close behind. Zac was dressed in his usual attire, khaki shorts, sandals and a t-shirt.

"Look at this guy," Zac said, pointing and laughing at Peter. "Who the hell does he think he is? Our travel agent?"

Peter looked at Zac and shook his head, almost in disgust and half pity. "You do know we're going somewhere cold. Might wanna put on something a little warmer."

Zac kicked his beat up old suitcase. "That's why I have this."

"Suit yourself," Peter sighed.

Will gave Peter a confused look, half surprised to see his good friend standing before him in the hangar.

"Not happy to see me?"

Will puzzled and wondered, "what are you doing here?"

Peter looked up, "getting this equipment loaded."

"Didn't know you were going?"

"Yeah, well someone up there has to know what they're doing."

"How many expeditions is this for you now?" Zac questioned.

Peter paused for a moment and gazed off into the distance. "This is lucky number thirteen, I believe. Hard to imagine it's been that many."

"And you've been the travel guide on each of them," Zac laughed, causing Will to crack a smile.

Peter nodded, "a very well compensated one at that. The way I see it, hopefully number fourteen will be to a warm island somewhere with a pristine, white sandy beach."

"That's what I'm talkin' about. Imagine the three of us lounging on the beach throwing back some beers. I can already see it," Zac said.

Peter looked both of them squarely in the eyes. "I need the two of you to focus, especially you," he said as he made eye contact again with Zac. "I need to talk to Will. Do you mind?"

"Actually I do, but what the hell, he's all yours," kidded Zac.

"How you holdin' up?"

"I'm good," Will replied, doing his best to muster a smile. "Like we say, new beginnings."

"Good, I'll see you on the plane then."

Will walked on with his luggage while Peter stayed back to move a large metal case into place on the plane.

"Excuse me," a voice from behind Peter said.

He turned around to see a beautiful woman standing before him. She was in her late twenties, tanned, with stunning, long, blond, hair pulled into a pony tail. She had holes in her jeans and scuffed tennis shoes. She pulled a small suitcase behind her and had a torn, black backpack strapped over her shoulder.

"Can I help you?" Peter asked in an authoritative, but helpful manner.

"I was told to look for, a, Peter."

He extended his hand. "You must be Liz, the zoology student."

"Are you Peter?"

He stuck his chest out, "Dr. Peter Miles, Director of Research and Chief Climatologist at the university."

"Sounds important."

"Only to those who don't know any better," he said.

She smiled, "so why make it sound that way?"

"It's all about appearance and how you present yourself. Most people are idiots. They think everything is formal and official, but it's not."

She stared at him with a rather bewildered look on her face.

"Take writing a book for example," he said. "The minute you publish it, most will take you for an expert on your subject, but all that it means is you were motivated enough to finish the damn project. You know, when I earned my Master's Degree I graduated with distinction."

Liz wasn't impressed. "Your point being?"

"The reason was because the program made our master's thesis an option for students, and I argued to the director of the program that all those that went ahead with the project should be allowed to graduate with distinction. Ever since then everyone has thought it was because I did well in school, when in reality it was because I had the balls to fight."

"You're pretty long winded and into yourself."

"Just confident."

Liz looked around, "um, I'm assuming that's the plane?"

"You assumed right."

She walked past him while cracking a phony, pseudo smile.

Hmmmm, Peter thought to himself.

Zac got his first full, unobstructed view of Liz as she approached them. He nudged Will several times, like that of a child trying desperately to get its parent's attention.

"Well, hello," Zac said as Liz finally made her way to them.

Zac moved in closer to Liz. "Can I take those for you?"

"Don't flatter yourself. I got it."

And with that she boarded the plane, leaving both of them in the dust.

Zac smiled, arms crossed, watching her board. "I like her already. Hell of a view, too."

A few seconds later they saw Chancellor Chee being followed closely by Jonathon. Chee walked briskly ahead, as Jonathon struggled with the luggage behind him. Both men were dressed in stunning, black suits and wore dark sunglasses.

Zac laughed for a moment. "Look at that moron pulling all the luggage."

Will motioned for Zac to cut it out, as Chee approached them. Liz and Peter joined the group, while Chee and his sidekick elegantly made their appearance at the hangar.

Chee removed his dark sunglasses to address the group, "gentlemen and lady, it is eighteen hundred hours."

Chapter Twelve

In what seemed like no time, the plane had ascended to a comfortable cruising altitude, and the group began to settle in to their new surroundings. Dobs and Brooks piloted the aircraft, though they appeared more like hired mercenaries. They were however, completely at ease behind the controls of the plane.

Never having been a big fan of flying, Will was finally able to breathe easier now that the plane had settled down and was free of turbulence. He was reading a thick, hardcover book that had a photo of Peter on the back, arms crossed, wearing a cardigan sweater. Will shook his head, perhaps giving off a slight hint of jealously.

Directly across the aisle from him was Zac who was holding one of the trade magazines about extreme sports. Will looked over at him and cracked a smile. Zac didn't notice him because he was staring in the direction of Liz, who was seated directly in front of Will.

Liz was writing on a sheet of paper. Under her feet was a book on polar bears. Her hair was pulled up, and in a knot, pierced with a pencil.

For that brief moment, Will stared in the direction of Zac, marveling at the fact that his good friend was completely enthralled with Liz and didn't even, for as much as a second, notice him.

Will chuckled. *He hasn't read a damn thing from that magazine*, he thought to himself.

A violent jolt suddenly hit the plane, ending the fearless innocence of the moment, sending Will into full-on-panic. He dropped the book into his lap and his entire body tightened. He could feel each muscle tense up and could hardly move. "God, I hate flying."

Zac laughed. "Relax, brother. Just some turbulence, nothin' more, nothin' less."

"Easy for you to say, you like flying. I, on the other hand, can't stand it; I'd rather come face to face with a mother polar bear defending her young."

Zac turned toward him. "It's not that I like flying, it's just that I'm not afraid. You gotta stop being afraid of things. Loosen up a bit. Take a shot of vodka. It'll calm the nerves."

Zac took a brief glance to where Liz was seated. "Watch this."

"Hey. . . book girl!"

Liz placed her book and notepad on her lap, and turned around.

"What about you," Zac asked. "Afraid of flyin'?"

"I don't get afraid," she confidently replied.

"Of flyin'?"

"Of anything," Liz boldly replied.

"She must have had two shots of vodka," Zac said, sitting back down in his seat.

Will shook his head. Zac got up from his seat, "nature calls." He walked rather briskly toward the back of the plane.

Will watched for a moment, chuckling softly to himself. His attention quickly focused back on Liz.

Will poked his head around the seat in front of him toward Liz, "don't mind him. He was part of the university's equal employment act."

She erupted with laughter, covering her mouth in embarrassment. "I know, right. With all these online schools these days, you never can be too certain. There was even that dean who fooled everyone into believing she had a doctorate. For some thirty years!"

Will nodded. "I read about that."

His eyes immediately focused on her notebook and books that were stacked at her feet. "Working on your dissertation?"

"Yeah," she replied while taking a quick scan of her notes. "On polar bears and the effect the climate has on them being a vulnerable species."

Will was quite impressed by the look of seriousness in her eyes. "An extremely important topic. I have no doubt you'll do it justice."

"I mean, think about a world without polar bears," Liz said. "I just can't fathom it. Or, a world where we have to tell our children about this fascinating place that once existed called, the Amazon."

Will nodded in agreement. "These are the topics that keep me up at night, one of the real reasons why I've shied away from having kids. Sometimes I'm not sure if this world is right for any more children to be born. So many problems and so little is being done."

She looked somewhat stunned. "But you do want to have kids, right? You look like you'd make a good father."

Will was a bit shaken by the statement. "Thanks. I do really want to have children. Just haven't found the right woman, I guess."

For what seemed like an eternity, but was no longer than a few seconds, their eyes met for a long and powerful understanding.

"Well," Will said, somewhat uncomfortable about what just occurred, "how about that thesis?"

"Right," she said smiling. "By taking samples of ice cores, we can tell what the climate was like in the past and analyze trends with the species in relation to that."

"Sounds fascinating," Will said, still leaning forward. "I'm sorry, I didn't even realize I'm leaning right into you."

She smiled. "I don't mind."

"Well, your work sounds fascinating," he said. "Much of my own work has centered on what you'll be encountering in yours."

"I know," she said. "I've read your publications and wanted you for my dissertation advisor, but you weren't accepting any new students this year."

Will let out a deep sigh of frustration and stared straight ahead. "I know. It's been a rough year."

"I'm sorry."

"Hey, what can you do, that's life sometimes."

She smiled at him.

"I really should be getting back to my seat."

She laughed, "right, it's quite a long walk back to your seat."

After a few seconds Will laughed as well, realizing that he was still in his seat. "Well I'll be right here if you need anything."

"Sounds good," she said as she turned around.

God, you're an idiot, he thought to himself.

Chapter Thirteen

Chee was seated next to the window while he meticulously sipped at his lemon tea. Jonathon looked up for a brief moment, and watched the steam, flowing up from the cup and past Chee's eyes. *Must be nice*, he thought to himself. *Just sit there and keep sipping that tea while I do all the real work. Jackass.*

Jonathon put his head down, and continued to type furiously at his laptop.

Behind Jonathon, sat Peter, who was energetically looking at his own laptop screen. Directly behind him stood Zac, busily stretching out his back and hamstrings.

"Can't you do that somewhere else?" Peter asked, as he turned around and got Zac's rear end, literally in his face. "God damn, that's a terrible view."

"Nope," Zac said as he popped back up. "You got all the space in the plane back here. Just stretching out the hammies."

"Well make it quick."

"What's on the screen there?" Zac asked.

"Just stretch," Peter replied.

Zac looked at him, not appreciating the curt tone, but decided to keep his cool and stretched down once more.

"All yours," he said, walking back to his seat.

Peter looked up for a brief moment, and then refocused his attention on the screen. He could feel the burden of the expedition weighing down on him. Everything rested on his lap, literally.

One thing at a time, he told himself. *Rome wasn't built in a day.*

"We'll find whatever it is that's out there," he whispered quietly to himself. "We'll find whatever's out there."

Chapter Fourteen

The plane continued onward through the crystal clear, blue sky, streaked with lines of dissipating clouds that crisscrossed and ran in all directions. The air was pristine and clear, a far cry from the civilized world.

Below, sat the enormous ice shelf, surrounded by thousands of small melting icebergs, remnants of what once was an enormous ice shield, remainders of a long forgotten past.

"Landing's gonna be tight," Dobs said.

Brooks looked down at the controls. "We'll circle a large area until we're clear of cracks and crevasses and the rest of all that shit."

"May have to land away from the designated area," Dobs replied.

Brooks gave Dobs a dubious glance. "He's not gonna like that."

Dobs tapped his fingers on the side of his seat. "Screw it. When he's in my plane, I'm the boss. Besides, the guy's a prick anyway. Who the hell does he think he is?"

Brooks cracked a smile. "A rich prick."

Dobs looked over, but didn't reply.

The plane descended sharply toward the ice shelf. The white sheet of ice rose like a towering form, a solid mass above the frigid, bitterly cold waters of the Canadian Arctic.

They all leaned to look out the windows at the ice shelf. Chee however, continued to sit, stoic, poised, and collected as always. He shot a disapproving look in the direction of Jonathon, who was busy marveling at the beauty of the landscape below, as if signaling him to sit back down in his seat.

Jonathon took one last glimpse out the window and then promptly returned to his seat, staring over at the others who were still admiring the beauty below.

Will and Liz could see calving off the side of the ice shelf. Large chunks of ice crashed and splashed into the icy blue water below, as the group continued to look on.

"It's breaking," Will blurted out.

"It's called calving," Zac chimed in from behind him.

The terrain below them was blanketed in solid white. It was at times blindingly reflective and discerning objects was difficult.

"Whoa," Will exclaimed.

"What is it?" Liz asked excitedly.

"Over there."

The group turned their heads and was greeted with one of the most amazing sights in the entire animal world.

On the ice below, moved a massive and regal polar bear. The giant creature was striding across the open landscape with a confidence that can only come from being the largest of all land predators.

"So different from the text book," Liz remarked, hardly able to contain the excitement that was building inside her.

"Yeah, those will eat you," Zac remarked from the back.

Liz turned around and shot him a sarcastic look.

Will shielded his eyes as the glare through the window was severe. "They won't be here much longer."

Zac threw his hands up in the air. "Oh God, here we go with this crap again."

"What?" Will asked.

"All this gloom and doom nonsense. You didn't ever listen to any of Michael Crichton's last interviews, did you?"

"No." he replied, not knowing quite where Zac was going with his point.

"Look, we can't predict the weather with certainty, right?"

"What's that got to do with anything?" Will asked.

Zac sighed. "Just answer the question. Are we able to predict what the temperature will be tomorrow to the exact degree?"

"Not really."

"My point exactly!" Zac earnestly replied. "That's what Crichton was getting at. How can we predict what the global climate will be like one hundred years from now? We can't. The same goes for what's happening here. Nobody knows for certain what will happen, and the same goes for the polar bear."

"Look, I agree with you, it's just…."

"Just what?" Zac asked.

"There are an overwhelming amount of scientists, many that have been featured on public radio, that say this land is doomed; and along with the melting will go the polar bear. They report this with terrible certainty."

Zac sighed. "Believe what you want. The only terrible certainty I know of is, thrash metal legends Kreator's, 1987 album, "Terrible Certainty."

"How do you listen to that stuff?"

"They're gods to the heavy metal world," Zac proudly announced.

"Dammit," Liz said, fuming.

Will turned to see what was the problem.

"While you two crazies were having your territorial pissoff, I got distracted for a second and lost track of the polar bear. I hope you two are happy."

"What?" Will asked, sounding dismayed, "we were having an academic debate."

"Sure. By talking about the metal band, Kreator?"

"So you've heard of 'em?" Zac asked, impressed by her heavy metal knowledge.

Liz nodded. "I've heard of all of them. My boyfriend was into that stuff. MegaDeath, Metallica, Slayer, Sepultura, Death, Cannibal Corpse, and the list goes on and on."

"Boyfriend?" Will asked.

Liz moved forward, standing only inches from Will's face. "Well, ex-boyfriend."

Will smiled nervously, his pulse quickened by Liz standing in such close proximity.

The two men, now with hearts and brains of teenagers, watched as she returned to her seat.

Chapter Fifteen

Dobs continued to scan below as Brooks methodically peered through a set of black binoculars.

Brooks moved forward slightly in his seat, "looks clear ahead."

"Well then," Dobs said, "let's lock that shit in."

Brooks shook his head and covered his nose. "Damn, when's the last time you showered?"

Dobs didn't even look over, rather just motioned his middle finger. "Might wanna let our friends back there know that we're landing. Gonna be a bumpy one."

Brook's voice crackled over the speakers. "Thank you for flying with us," he said coughing. "We'll be landing shortly, please return to your seats. We know you have a choice when it comes to private aviation, and we hope you will choose us in the future."

The group returned to their seats, having a hard time holding back the laughter. Will and Zac glanced over at one another, knowing full well what the other was thinking.

"Those two guys," Zac said, shaking his head, "where'd they find them? They wouldn't know class if it smacked them right in the ass."

They quickly fumbled to their seats, locking in their seat belts just as the plane hit the ice, hard. It skidded, vibrated, and shook intensely, making its way over the wide open expanse of ice.

Will's body was stiff with fear, as Zac looked over at him and laughed. "How 'bout that shot of vodka!" He shouted over the roar of the engine.

Will's eyes remained transfixed on the seat in front of him as the plane continued its violent landing. Finally, and to the relief of everyone, it came to a stop. Will remained rigid, with his hands still firmly gripping his seat.

Liz's head popped over the top of the seat in front of him. "You can let go now. By the looks of it you've got a real stranglehold on that seat."

Will embarrassed, looked down at his hands, white, from the death grip that he had on his seat. He slowly released his hands. "Guess I got carried away."

Liz smiled, but turned away so Will wouldn't see her expression.

Chapter Sixteen

Outside, the cold winds and icy world awaited the eager group. As they exited the plane, they could hear the wind rushing and screeching past the body of the plane.

Will looked up ahead at Zac and reached out at his shoulder to grab him. "Do me a favor. Please put some warmer clothes on. You're wearing shorts and a t-shirt. We're not in the Bahamas just yet."

Zac shook his head and reached down into his bag. "Yes mother!"

Brooks paced back and forth examining every inch of the plane for any possible damage from their harder-than-anticipated landing. He spat dark tobacco juice, instantly staining the pristine, white ice below.

"Thought you said we was clear," Dobs said, stretching his sore back.

Brooks marched over to Dobs. "Get off my back and learn proper English, you dumb fool!"

Dobs took no time in delivering a blow to the face of Brooks, causing the man to stumble backward. Brooks touched his face as he regained his balance; it was evident that he was bleeding, from the spots of blood on the ice.

Brooks steamrolled straight into Dobs, sending both men sprawling onto the ice.

"Gentlemen!" Chee shouted, catching the two men by surprise. "Time is of the essence."

Chee was now dressed in warmer clothing, including a fur, hooded coat, gloves, and snow boots. As was his custom, he looked flawless, impeccable.

"We are ten miles from our landing coordinates." Chee stated.

Chee moved in closer to have a look at the landing gear. "Can we take off?"

"Fixable," Dobs said, wincing in pain from the blow delivered by Brooks to his chest. "We just need time."

"Of which we have very little," Chee replied, already with his back toward Dobs, he strode away, hands behind his back. "Stay behind and make the necessary repairs, but be ready to fly out. You have twelve hours, Mr. Jackson. Is that understood?"

"Yup," Dobs replied, shaking his head back and forth.

Chapter Seventeen

The cold chill quickly filled the plane's interior thanks to the long back ramp being opened for the unloading of the snowmobiles. The crew knew time was the enemy, but the elements were not kind either.

"Let's get going people!" Peter shouted. "We're wasting valuable time. Everyone should be doing something right now, and if you have nothing to do, come find me, and I'll find something for you to do!"

Zac's eyes met Jonathon's and was drawn into following the assistant to the back of the plane. The two stopped at the area where the snowmobiles were stored. One by one, they would have to unload the vehicles that would be their main lines of transportation throughout new and unfamiliar surroundings.

Jonathon stopped what he was doing and watched Zac, who was hard at work trying to free the items that had fallen around one of the snowmobiles at the back of the plane.

"You're doing that all wrong," Jonathon snidely remarked.

"What?"

Jonathon folded his arms and let out a long and drawn out sigh. "I said, you're doing that all wrong."

Zac shook his head and chuckled to himself. "How would you know? It'll be fine. It's not rocket science."

Jonathon threw his hands up in the air and began to pace. "Look, we have to do it the way the Chancellor wants. Get it?"

Zac had gathered a large quantity of food and travel supplies in his hands; He set them down on the floor and approached Jonathon. "Look, I don't know when you lost your balls, but start thinkin' for yourself for a change. Quit kissin' ass, and be your own man."

A look of shock and embarrassment began to brew on Jonathon's face, as if it was quite possible that no one had ever been that straightforward with him. He quickly turned around and headed away from Zac.

Zac stood there with an exasperated look on his face. *What a tool,* he thought to himself.

Chapter Eighteen

Peter was sitting comfortably in the driver seat of the elevated, red, ice vehicle that sat three, as he made his way onto the ramp at the back of the plane. The small cabin had two seats in the front and one seat in the back. The entire cabin was enclosed by glass, and the base of the vehicle had three ski runners that supported it with a propeller on the back. It was fully equipped to make its way through barren and isolated habitats.

Will stopped for a moment to check out the vehicle as Peter was moving by. It was impressive indeed.

The driver side window rolled down.

"Everything we can carry on the snowmobiles, plus fuel. We'll set up camp ten miles from here!" Peter yelled.

Will nodded, not bothering to reply, as the hum from the vehicle was far too loud to try and shout over. *I value my vocal chords.*

While trying to regain his hearing, Will opened the first door back inside the cabin of the plane. *It's absolutely frigid out there,* he thought to himself.

To his surprise, the compartment wasn't empty. Liz stood half naked as the door opened.

Will instantly looked away. "Oh my God, I'm so sorry."

Liz was in her bra and snow pants; tan skin against the white.

Liz was amused by how squeamish and awkward he seemed. "What's the matter? Never seen a female body before?" She asked, while putting on her shirt.

Will unable to respond, body almost frozen, stared out the window with the most expressionless of stares.

"You're a difficult one to read," she said, finishing dressing with a fur coat.

"Is it okay to look?" Will asked.

"Yep," she replied.

As Will slowly turned his head, Liz screamed, "not yet!"

Will instinctively put his hands to his face, as Liz let out a good-sized laugh. "I'm just teasing."

Slowly, Will's hands came down from his eyes. "Look, I shouldn't be in here. I'll be outside."

Will turned and made his way to the door. To his surprise Liz said, in an apologetic tone, "no, stay."

He turned around, surprised.

"Sit down, you're making me nervous, and for cryin' out loud, stop looking like a scared puppy dog."

Will had a seat in the chair that was closest to the door.

"Ever think you selected the wrong path in life? Regretted most of your decisions?" Will blurted out.

Liz paused for a second while she finished lacing her boot, "what in the world brings that on?"

"Don't know. Just a lot of thoughts going through my head."

Liz moved a few steps closer to Will. "Will, it's okay to look in my direction. I'm dressed now."

Will had been staring blankly out the window, but he turned and then met her eyes.

"To answer your question," she said as she sat down next to him, "I don't have any regrets. Not one."

Will seemed a bit awkward at first, not quite knowing where to put his hands. Finally, he rested them firmly in his lap. "Any regrets about selecting zoology for your major?"

Liz smiled. "Glad I made that choice."

"Not much need for zoology professors these days. Well, at least the university doesn't need them."

"To me it's about helping people. Research. Finding solutions to help solve problems through that research. You don't need to be teaching to do that!"

She stood up as Will looked on, very intrigued by her demeanor and poise.

Liz turned around. "And it's all in the attitude."

Will sat there wondering for a moment, and completely enthralled with what he had just heard from Liz. Slowly he got to his feet, but was nearly startled out of his skin by human, agonized, screaming and vicious, snarling sounds. He headed straight for the door.

Outside Dobs was sprawled out on the ice, blood running everywhere.

For a second, Will looked around, completely disoriented at what was taking place. It all seemed to be happening in slow motion.

Brooks ran over to aid his fallen comrade, desperate to rescue him from the grip of the wolf. He aimed a kick at the wolf, causing the animal to snap viciously at him.

"Outta here!" Brooks shouted, trying to intimidate the creature, but it was no use as it tore into Dob's leg.

The wolf savagely ripped his right pant leg, clean off. Its sheer power and ferocity startled everyone, as the animal mauled Dobs.

Lying face down and completely helpless, Dobs screamed in terror as the animal tore his left calf wide open, exposing the muscle.

The weight of the wolf kept Dobs firmly planted, with his face to the ground. He felt himself on the edge of consciousness when suddenly, his rescue finally came.

Bam!

The sound of gunfire pierced the screaming and snarling.

Bam!

Once more gunfire echoed, and Will looked over his shoulder to see Peter aiming squarely at the wolf.

The injured animal had run some thirty yards away, fallen, and then staggered up once more. Peter followed, stopped, steadied himself, and fired one last shot.

Bam!

The wolf instantly fell to the ground. Its body lay there. Will ran toward Dobs while Peter raced out to the dead carcass. Before Will could even get to Dobs, Liz was already there, assessing his injuries.

"Get me the first aid kit," she shouted, bending down to look at the leg. "You're lucky," though she realized his leg would most likely never be the same.

Dobs, still prone, muttered through gritted teeth, "somehow, I don't feel so lucky."

Liz looked up at Will. "Where's the first aid?"

"Zac's getting it."

"It better be an advanced kit! He needs morphine," she replied, as she tried to check his other leg for injuries.

"Easy there," Dobs muttered.

"You want me to help you or not?"

He didn't reply, rather he kept his head down and moaned.

"Great, it's the advanced kit," Liz said, as Zac returned.

She tore open the kit and threw several items onto the ice. She worked quickly to treat the lacerations.

"Are you qualified to administer those types of shots?" Zac asked.

Liz already had the syringe held in her mouth and was busy stretching on the gloves. "I've worked as an E.M.T. with the county for two years," she managed to say.

She injected Dobs with a shot of morphine and an antibiotic. Both Will and Zac cringed as she administered the injections.

"Damn woman, can you be any more violent?" Dobs mumbled.

She finished the injections and discarded the needles in the sharps container and snapped it shut. "You're lucky I have this to administer."

Will peered down at both of them. "Is he going to make it?"

Liz nodded. "That shot of morphine should do the trick, ease the pain a bit, plus an antibiotic. Good thing you'll be flying back soon."

Finally Peter returned, and he wasn't alone.

Chapter Nineteen

Slung over Peter's shoulder were the grizzly remains of the wolf that had only minutes prior viciously mauled Dobs on the ice. Its limp and lifeless body was stained red with blood and had already begun to smell. The odor was overwhelming, as everyone began to cough and gag.

"God, man, get that outta here!" Zac said, taking several steps back while covering his nose. "It smells worse than shit!"

Peter paid no attention to Zac, as he coldly stared down at Dobs who was still lying on the ice. "We need to get moving people."

Liz looked up at Peter with a look of disbelief. "Excuse me? We had an injury. Give us a second, okay."

"We don't have a second, people. Let's get moving now," Peter fired back.

He swung his shoulders in the direction of Will and Zac, bringing the dead wolf very close to them. They both flinched backward.

"Like I said, get that damn thing outta here!" Zac yelled.

Peter gave Zac a serious stare, eye to eye. "This is food."

Zac laughed, as Will looked on seriously.

"I never said anything about it being for us," Peter said.

His tone was at a level of intensity that neither Zac nor Will had heard before, and it especially startled Will.

The entire crew appeared confused, especially Will, whose mind was busy digesting what he had just heard.

"Bait, Mr. Freeman, bait," Chee said, coming out of nowhere.

Everything fell silent for a moment, no one knowing quite what to say.

"We move now!" Peter said in a loud and authoritative voice. He glanced over in the direction of Dobs. "He's a big boy. He can fend for himself."

Zac shot Peter a confused look. "Chill, man. Give us a moment. Someone was just hurt, okay."

Peter approached Zac with the shotgun in his left hand, and the wolf slumped over his right shoulder. "There's a lot at stake out here. We must now begin the search for the creature. I'm not going to say it again. Let's get moving, people."

Chapter Twenty

The three snowmobiles raced across the wide-open, white terrain, their tracks crisscrossing in all directions, leaving a confusing pattern of lines.

Zac looped in and out, cutting Will off from time-to-time, laughing with the enthusiasm of a child the entire time.

Will glanced over at his good friend who was now at his side. He shook his head and smiled. In some respects he envied the carefree spirit of Zac as he sped off again, turning back around and shouting out something that was indecipherable.

Will could hear the ice vehicle following closely behind at his back, with Peter at the helm of the machine. The constant whine of the snowmobile and the drone of the ice vehicle reminded him of the sounds of progress, if there was such a thing. Progress not only in life, but in the search for an elusive beast. *Is it really out there?*

"Woo hoo!" Zac shouted as he zoomed in and around Will, breaking into his thoughts.

Zac performed a display of risky moves, circling several times around Will, putting the snowmobile to the extreme test before accelerating a considerable distance ahead.

Damn X gamer, Will thought to himself.

Peter, from the large vehicle watched Zac, the adrenaline junkie, leap several open crevasses and get airborne, to staggering heights. He shook his head, as his eyes focused in on the terrain ahead. "Fucking idiot's going to get himself killed."

Jonathon, seated directly behind Peter, snorted in laughter with his eyes still glued to his laptop.

Peter sneaked a glance at Jonathon in the rear view mirror. The assistant was furiously typing on his laptop. *Another idiot we got here,* he thought to himself. His eyes once more returned to the open terrain ahead of him. For a moment he allowed his mind to wander to a bigger, better, and more fruitful future.

Not for one second did he trust Chee, and he absolutely despised Jonathon. Both of them repulsed him, but the fact that Chee had been willing to deposit a cool $100,000 into one of Peter's many offshore bank accounts, even before they even set foot on the ice shelf, made him believe that this was indeed, a worthwhile endeavor.

With compensation that neared $1,000,000 for successful capture of one of the creatures, and an added $50,000 per creature, dead or alive, Peter had plans. He planned to use the money as his safety blanket to allow him to quit his main career in teaching and launch several profit potential companies, pen a few follow-up books to his first best-seller, and live the downright good life.

He needed this expedition to succeed at all costs. He wanted to retire from teaching to focus on his writing and other profitable revenues. At the age of thirty-six, he felt he had already been part of the day-to-day grind for far too long. Nothing was going to get in his way.

He blinked, bringing his attention back to the ice shelf.

Chapter Twenty-One

Dobs lay on his cot. *Am I drunk?*

He propped himself up on the edge of the bed, trying to remember recent events. It had been almost one year since he had touched a drop of alcohol, completely clean by his own admission, though it had cost him his first marriage.

A quick scan of the floor and surroundings didn't reveal cans or bottles. He pushed himself away from the cot. Slowly he took steps, one in front of the other.

The shooting pain in his left leg caused the memories to come flashing back. The image of the wolf attack was now replaying in his mind. He looked down at his left calf, wrapped with white bandages.

"Oh," he said, cringing in pain and hunching over. *Maybe I need that drink.*

He was relieved that his equilibrium and haziness weren't due to alcohol consumption, but rather to his chance encounter with a lone wolf. However, the pain from his leg did little to calm his solitary thoughts. Miraculously, he was able to limp slowly toward the rear of the plane, his left leg dragging considerably.

"Brooks?"

He paused for a moment, expecting to hear his buddy shout back. Silence prevailed.

"Hey Brooks, stop messin' around and get out here!" Dobs shouted.

Again, only silence.

Dobs continued to limp toward the rear of the plane, finally reaching the lever that slowly lowered the back ramp of the plane. A gust of wind entered, chilling him significantly, but his jacket was back on the cot, and he didn't have the strength to go back for it. Awkwardly, he made his way down the ramp and eventually onto the ice.

He saw Brooks's dark tobacco juice spittle on the ice and was comforted as he imagined he'd find him nearby. He looked at the tobacco stains for several seconds before other features caught his attention. Some of this was blood!

Farther ahead, large pools of blood were everywhere. The ice was splattered with it. His eyes quickly darted back and forth, taking in as much as he could comprehend. *Damn wolf, got me better than I thought.*

Then he paused for a moment, remembering that the encounter with the wolf had occurred much earlier in the day, possibly some four to five hours ago. This blood was fresh, and he remembered, the wolf was dead.

Instantly the hair on his body stood on end, his senses heightened, as he looked up from staring at the ice. Slowly, he turned around, half expecting someone or something to come charging full speed at him. All was deathly still.

Chapter Twenty-Two

The snowmobiles were parked close to a red tent. The sides of the tent rippled and flapped back and forth in the wind. It was small but snug, and it provided a safe haven from the fierce elements that appeared to be getting worse by the hour.

Will and Liz knelt near the small fire close to the entrance to the red tent. They were trying to plot their exact location. Liz hovered, in great anticipation, as Will squinted to get the correct readings.

"Anything?" Liz asked with excitement.

Will squinted again, "might be time for glasses for me." He moved his head back a few inches. "There we go. I was starting to think that my vision was going. Big problem in my family. Everyone seems to go blind."

"Will!"

"What?"

"The readings, if you don't mind," Liz said playfully.

"Right."

No sooner had Will spoken, when something hard and firm smashed into the side of his head. It stung, rendering him speechless for a brief moment.

He swung around slowly to see the figure of Zac standing proudly grinning with another snowball in his hand. "Bulls-eye!"

Will stared at him for a brief moment, and then gently began to rub his head. "Get over here! This is your area of expertise."

Zac stood, arms crossed against his muscular chest. "My expertise is cash. Half a million to be exact," he reported in an affected, cool manner.

Will shook his head. "How you ever earned your Ph.D is beyond me. One of those on-line schools, right?"

Liz laughed out loud, as Zac waved his middle finger toward his good friend.

Will quickly then turned back to the task-at-hand, examining the screen. "These numbers are different from what's on record."

Liz could also see the screen, "furthering the evidence of global warming."

"You're right," Will said, "the only question is, are we humans contributing to it?"

Zac was now kneeling with the two, "see, this is why I like this guy. He makes you think. He always leaves you with something to think about."

Will looked at Zac, somewhat surprised by what his friend had said. He was quite pleased by the compliment. "Thanks."

"Just one question?" Zac asked.

"Sure, what is it?"

"What were you talking about again?"

Chapter Twenty-Three

Dobs scanned the horizon for anything at all. Anything he may have missed. Only white, and more white was all he saw.

He limped past the large amounts of blood on the ice, and slowly made his way back to the plane, his left foot touching the bottom of the ramp, still in pain. He craned his neck around to have another look around him. *Gotta stop watchin' all those slasher films. They got me paranoid.*

He saw nothing but the unchanged whiteness of the expanse. Slowly he trudged his way up the ramp, stopping at the top to catch his breath.

"Brooks, if you're hiding inside!" he shouted. "If you're hiding in there making my immobile ass go on a wild goose chase lookin' for you, I'm gonna open a can on your ass when I find ya!"

He half expected, half feared, that Brooks would burst from some unseen vantage point; but there was only silence and the ever present whipping of the wind.

With much difficulty, he managed to bend down and begin urgently searching through the luggage that was still on the floor. "Gotta be here somewhere."

He finally found what he had been looking for, a red satellite phone. He began dialing.

"Pick up. Pick up, god dammit! Pick up!"

The phone rang and rang until finally a voice on the other line answered.

"Yes?" the voice asked.

"Who is this?" Dobs asked.

"This is Jonathon. You called me."

"I need to talk to the chief."

"The Chancellor isn't available right now. Tell me what this is about, and I'll relay the message to him."

Dobs sighed out loud. "I need him now. Get him dammit!"

"Well," Jonathon calmly replied, "as I said, he's not available. If there's something you wish to tell him, I can give him the message. Otherwise, you're wasting my time and his."

"It's a god damn logistical issue, relaying messages won't work!"

Logistical, big word for an idiot, Jonathon thought to himself.

Dobs could hear Jonathon communicating with two people in the background. For a minute he tried to listen in on their conversation, but then Jonathon laid the phone down on his lap.

"Who is it?" Peter asked.

Jonathon covered the receiver, "the guy from the plane." He slowly brought the phone back to his ear, pausing for a moment, as if struggling with the words. "The Chancellor made himself very clear. Twelve hours, no excuses. Fix it." He hung up the phone without even giving Dobs the opportunity to give a response.

"Son of a bitch!" Dobs cursed, slamming the phone to the floor.

He picked it up again and began to redial, but it was now badly damaged. A sound caught Dobs by surprise from somewhere near the back of the plane. Silently, he pulled his handgun from his side holster, and began to limp forward, one painful step at a time. He paused for a moment, turning to his left when something caught his attention.

His weapon was aimed squarely at the bags of luggage piled several feet high. Trying his best to steady his hand, it continued to shake badly. Several seconds passed before the predator finally showed himself. A giant rat scurried along the floor making its way to the open hatch. Dobs stared at it for a moment, and let out a chuckle. An overwhelming sense of relief came over him. "A rat, a god damn rat!"

No sooner had his fear been eased when a noise possibly from one of the large storage compartments began.

"What now?"

He turned, not quite sure at first, from where the noise was coming. He peered at a storage container that was wide open in the front, but it was pitch black inside and impossible to see. *This shitty plane is crawling with rats.*

His hair suddenly stood on end. Returning his stare were, a set of glowing red eyes, much larger than any rat's eyes.

Chapter Twenty-Four

"That storm's going to hit us in two days, not four," Peter said, approaching the group huddled around the laptop. Chee and Jonathon followed closely behind. Nearby, the core sample rod was shoved into the ice.

Chee stepped closer to Peter, "you just make sure that we find what we have come all this way for, Mr. Miles."

Peter paused for a second, checking the time on his wristwatch. "Let's move out. Everyone up."

Zac watched Peter for a moment. "Can you give us a second? We're trying to get some readings. This is what we've come all this way for."

Peter was already leaving the group. He stopped, paused for a moment, and then turned around. "That's funny. All I saw earlier was your ass throwing snowballs like a little kid." He pointed toward the laptop, "and that, isn't what we came all this way for."

Chapter Twenty-Five

Dobs looked on, as his body remained frozen in place. The glowing red eyes sprung forth from the darkness, as a creature leaped out of the confined hiding space, showing its true power and mass. The juvenile creature was blanketed in shaggy white fur, a miniature version of the gigantic adults of its species. It was built nearly identically to modern day gorillas, with a powerful body and impressively strong front limbs and back legs. The nose was sunken in, much like a pit-bull, giving it the most fearsome of appearances. Accompanying this pit-bull like appearance were two enormous fangs that protruded downward from the back of the mouth. These were the weapons that the species used to deliver the fatal bite. Dobs turned to run. He screamed in agony, as the creature sunk its massive claws deep into his back, ripping his flesh wide open and gouging out massive hunks of flesh.

Dobs could feel the creature's weight upon him as the creature pinned him to the floor.

The pain was excruciating while the animal savagely ripped into him. The animal let out all sorts of shrieks and snarls, as it went about its grizzly task, of literally stripping flesh and muscle from bone.

Dobs tried to cry out, but it was no use. He felt himself on the verge of unconsciousness as a result of the massive amounts of blood that he had lost.

Just then, out of the corner of his eye, he spotted a snow pick lying on the floor. He reached his left hand toward it, falling short of the pick by several inches.

He lay there helpless, at the mercy of the creature that was quickly working its way deeper and deeper into his exposed back and legs. Then with every ounce of energy he could muster, he made one last shaky stretch with his left arm toward the pick. His hand touched down on the back of the pick.

Miraculously, he we was able to swing his left hand with the ice pick, directly at his attacker. The creature let out a howling cry, as the first attempt sent the ice pick directly into its left arm. Dobs stabbed the creature frantically, all of this happening in a whirl.

Dobs stabbed at it one last time, and could see the figure above him, literally step right over him and out of view. He heard it gallop off into the distance, and make its way out onto the open ice.

Dobs lay there with his head on the floor. *No pain, I feel nothing.* He was breathing calmly, to his surprise, and wasn't feeling any lightheadedness or faintness.

He turned his head to look at the damage, expecting to see the floor bathed in blood. However, all was remarkably clean with a few random blood stains here and there. *Guess I'm tougher than I thought.*

As he was about to lower himself back to the floor to rest he saw something horrifying. It was so inconceivable, no one could be prepared.

Chapter Twenty-Six

"North, why are we heading north?" Zac demanded from the others, as Peter had slipped away. "Our data is right here."

Will was busy wrapping up various cords for the computer and stuffed them neatly into his backpack. "I agree, but obviously they don't."

Jonathon was also busy, gathering all of Chee's belongings, and overheard them. "Move it, you two," he said, as he hurried by, racing to catch up with Peter.

Zac held up his hand, pretending a backhand at Jonathon's face, causing Will to crack a smile.

"You, of all people," Will said, "wanting to stay and do research. I must say I'm impressed."

Zac smiled, "look, I know around campus I'm thought of as the hip professor, but I understand the importance of why we're here. Global climatic change isn't on the forefront of everyone's minds, but maybe it should be."

Liz listened in, curious where the conversation was going.

"How can you convince a single mother of two, just struggling to get by, that the rainforests of the world, or the melting glaciers are important?" Zac asked.

"You're asking me?" Will inquired.

"The answer to that question is one that every scientist, fighting for this cause, is wrestling with, day in and day out," Zac added while pacing back and forth.

Will glanced over at Liz who appeared captivated and waiting for the next words that would come from Zac. Oddly, he had the same feeling.

"Feeling empathy," Zac added, and paused, as if he himself had spent many a night grappling with the very topic he was discussing. "Empathy for what you haven't seen or will only see through the media is difficult to cultivate. Think about how many folks will ever get to come to a place like this, witness its raw power, stand on ice that is timeless. The answer isn't many. People are immersed in their own lives, trying to make a living, and provide a good life for their children. And I don't blame them one bit. Life is hard, especially with the way the economy is going these days. It's hard to push public awareness for issues such as overfishing. I do think we have failed, not failed as a society, but failed as humanity. We must find a way to tie everything together."

Will couldn't remember the last time he had been so impressed by a speech. Zac scratched his head at the slight stubble that had begun growing on his usually immaculate, polished bald head. "The answer to all of this lies in a term called, geologic connection. It has the power to unite us all."

"Geologic connection?" Will asked.

Zac nodded. "The idea's that, the geologic timeline of life, connects us all. It has the power to bring us all together. Often times paleontologists say the one thing that keeps them all going, is this idea of the geologic connection they feel toward their work. It's the idea that someone can pick up a fossil that is one hundred million years old, and be the first living organism to see it in as many years. It can make us all care about one another, even people and places we will never meet or see because we are all part of the geologic timeline of life. Regardless of race, color, or religion, no one can deny all of our places in the history of Earth."

Will stood there with a grin as wide as his face, clapping and clapping. Liz joined in, and for several seconds, Zac took many curtain calls, bowing to his faithful audience.

A loud whistle pierced the air. The crew could see Peter standing some distance away. He motioned impatiently.

"Party's over," Will said as they all began heading toward Peter. "We march on."

Zac brought up the rear. "God damn death march if you ask me."

Chapter Twenty-Seven

Dobs began to shake violently after his discovery. He began to scream. Louder and louder. His agonized screams would have been enough to alert anyone in sight, had he not been in the middle of nowhere. He screamed uncontrollably, as the sight of his missing legs seared into his brain.

"They gone," he barely whispered, still not believing fully what he was seeing. "They gone!" he said again, now going into shock.

He searched with his eyes but was repulsed by the thought that he would see his legs lying somewhere in a dark pool of blood. He did not see them.

Suddenly, a horrific rush of pain came upon him that sent him into convulsions. His body went rigid, then he began to violently shake. *Must raise head,* he thought, as he began to choke and vomit blood. Blood now was everywhere. Suddenly, the shaking stopped. Abruptly his agonized moaning ended. It was over. Dobs was dead.

Chapter Twenty-Eight

"What took you so long?" Peter demanded as the group approached where he, Jonathan and Chee were making preparations for moving ahead.

Zac was about to open his mouth, but Peter cut him off, "save it," he said, dismissing him with his hand. "I don't give a damn. We must be quick."

Zac allowed his gaze to drift upwards, to watch the cloud formations passing by in the wind. Peter made direct eye contact with him. "Look, I could care less if you don't listen to me, but know this, if the elements don't kill you, the wolves, polar bears, or whatever else is crawling around this place will kill you. If you get killed, that's one less man on this expedition. Understood?"

Zac saluted him. "Aye, aye, captain."

Peter stood in front of the group as the blistery cold wind battered them continually. "Make sure you have your satellite phones and G.P.S. with you at all times. Take enough food and water to hold you over until we find what we're looking for. Maximum two days, but we'll aim for one."

Like a child who had just found his father's gun, Jonathon held up the Ground Penetrating Radar to have a full view of it. He scanned the entire length of the device, every crevice, gadget, button and lever.

"We can use the Ground Penetrating Radar that Vanna White over there is currently modeling for us," Peter remarked. "Use them over the surface. We're looking for remains, not fossils. These things will pick up bones that have recently been laid down, remains of any sorts, or hopefully what we're searching for. Are there any questions?"

Zac raised his hand.

Peter acknowledged him. "What is it?"

"If we find bottle caps or loose change, can we keep it?"

Peter agitatedly cleared his throat. "As I was saying, these Ground Penetrating Radars or G.P.R.'s could make or break the expedition. Conditions will become bleak and visibility might be inches in front of your face. We must use this tool to our advantage."

Jonathon was now resting the G.P.R. squarely on the ice, being quite careful not to damage the expensive piece of technology. "Where will these work best?" asked Jonathan.

"Excellent question," Peter replied.

Jonathon smirked causing Zac to roll his eyes. Peter grabbed the G.P.R. from Jonathon to show the group. "You can use these over an open crevasse if you encounter one. Most importantly, stick to the coordinates that we have mapped out. Our best guess is that we are looking for something that is from the primate family."

Liz shot a brief glance at Will, "how big is this thing?" she asked.

"Let us do the worrying, babe," Peter replied.

Will restrained Liz, as her body lunged toward Peter.

"Your boyfriend's here to protect you," Peter laughed.

Will said nothing, as Liz shot Peter a fierce glare. He continued to hold her back by the waist. With his hands around her, he slowly continued to inch her backward and away from Peter.

"It's bigger than a polar bear," he whispered into her ear.

Despite the fury coursing through her veins, she felt a certain comfort being in Will's arms. It was comfort she hadn't felt in a long time, maybe a comfort she hadn't ever experienced.

Chapter Twenty-Nine

The plane was quiet, as if the struggle between Dobs and the dreadful creature hadn't taken place. A closer look revealed a trail of blood leading down the plane's back ramp. Dobs's upper body was nowhere to be found.

Half a mile away, his now pale-white face blended in with the ice and snow. His torso was completely exposed on the wide open terrain. The wind and snow tangled his long hair.

Slowly, a wolf approached out of the dense fog that was forming. The animal approached the body with caution. It nudged at the right hand, pushing it back and forth and then stepping back a few paces.

As the wolf was about to make its way back to claim his meal, he sensed something wasn't right. Instinctively, his senses heightened, as he studied his surroundings for a moment, carefully calculating the situation. Then, it quickly darted away, into the fog.

A majestic and almost regal in stature, full-grown, adult polar bear approached the remains. The animal examined the body carefully. A sound from somewhere out in the fog also caught his attention. The bear put his foot down on the body and roared menacingly, announcing to the world that this was his property.

The bear waited for a moment, senses heightened and with its ears alert for even the slightest movement or sound from nearby.

Then, one after another, a steady chorus of shrieks and an ungodly, piercing howl began from somewhere inside the veil of fog. On and on the horrible sounds continued. The bear once again let out a cry of its own, planting his foot over the body of the dead man, crushing him beneath his weight.

All of a sudden, the bear charged off into the fog. It ran, now fully grasping his own peril, as the sounds and shrieks began converging upon him. Sounds swirled about in the fog as he made his way further away from the body. Suddenly the bear came to a complete stop, breathing heavily in the blinding fog, as the noises began to converge upon him.

Chapter Thirty

"You three," Peter said, pointing to Will, Zac, and Liz, "take the northwest cliff, and we'll cover the surface. That damn thing's out there, I think we all know it."

Peter tried to scan the horizon, as visibility had once again become difficult with the pockets of fog continuing to billow. He made direct eye contact with the group. "We want this thing or things dead or alive. Preferably alive though. Any questions?"

Liz leaned back into Will and whispered. "Things?"

Will nudged close to her ear. "I'll explain later."

Peter noticed the two. "You two have any questions?"

Before Will could even reply, Chee interjected. "No questions, Mr. Miles. Time is of the essence."

Peter nodded, as if agreeing with the statement. "Then what are we waiting for? Let's get moving."

Peter, Chee, and Jonathon headed in the opposite direction from the others.

"Things?" Liz repeated to Will. He pulled her aside, far away from the others. "Yeah, I didn't want to say anything, but I've already noticed a few tracks."

She appeared uneasy. "Please tell me they were polar bear tracks."

Will shook his head and hesitated for a moment, as if harboring the great secret of all secrets. "Well," he took a deep breath, "look, I didn't want to say anything back there for fear of scaring you and Zac, and I didn't want to alert the goon squad that their hypothesis seems to be correct."

Liz's eyes widened. "So, it's true? There's something real out here?" Her voice was now somewhat shaky and wobbly, a far cry from the confident and sturdy-as-a-rock demeanor that she always projected.

"Something massive," Will replied, "more than one."

Liz appeared confused and leaned in to cross-examine him. Will moved in closer as well. "I've seen multiple sets of tracks. It's highly unlikely that just one individual did this. There's nothing on this ice that would produce such enormous tracks."

"Okay, now you really have me freaked out. So, you're saying there's more than one of these things running around. Isn't it possible one of them could account for several sets of tracks?"

Will shook his head, seeming somewhat disappointed by the notion that he was indeed correct. "I was hoping for the same thing, but I'm afraid we're wrong. There isn't just one out here. There's more. The tracks are from various-sized individuals. They're circling us, corralling us into a position where we're most vulnerable, where we're an easy kill for them. We're being hunted."

Chapter Thirty-One

The polar bear sped madly out to the open. His huge padded feet made very little noise while he bounded over the ice. Instinctively, his mind said to run, but his senses were on overload, running into the fog. The hideous noises and sounds continued to draw closer.

A massive arm emerged, and delivered a crushing blow to the right side of the bear's skull, sending him smashing down to the ice. He slid for several feet across the slippery surface. When he finally came to a stop, he lay there for a moment and then groggily stumbled to his feet.

The bear let out a preemptive roar, though it resembled more of a cry for help than one of dominance. Intimidated and injured with a severe blow to the side of its head, he stood there helpless as the chorus of insane cries began to close in upon him.

Something whizzed by him on the left, causing him to swipe with his massive paw at the shape, but it disappeared quickly into the fog. He was instantly hit on his right side by something hard and forceful. The blow struck his chest, causing him to once again be sent to the ice.

A second attacker came thundering in on four powerful legs and bit down with powerful, oversized jaws directly into the polar bear's already damaged skull. The first attacker then began violently ripping into the animal's abdomen. Soon all sounds and shrieks centered upon the scene of the dying animal, as he let out his final death cry.

The fog effectively erased all evidence.

Chapter Thirty-Two

In an instant apparent of madness, Will began to charge toward Peter and Chee. Liz looked over at Zac, who was also watching his friend storm across the ice.

"You lied to us!" Will accused, breathing heavily, coming to a halt.

Peter looked up from busily informing Chee and Jonathon of the game plan.

"What the hell are you talking about?"

"I'm talking about research and our chance to do just that out here. It was agreed that we would be able to implement the research necessary to save our respective programs."

Peter laid down his bag and approached Will. "And you've done just that."

"That's crap, and you know it. We need more time."

Will's tone and harshness startled Chee. The Chancellor looked toward Will.

"Look, Will, keep your mouth shut. Now's not the time to push the envelope with me. The stakes are too high out here."

It was too late though. Chee had overheard the confrontation and had made his way over to investigate. "Is there a problem, Mr. Miles?"

"No problem," Peter replied as his eyes bored into Will, not even bothering to look over at Chee.

"The hell there isn't a problem," Will said, staring Chee straight in the eyes. "We were promised research, and so far we've done very little of that."

"Mr. Freeman," Chee said defiantly, as he came striding toward him with his hands clasped behind his back. "We have a very big task ahead of us. A great opportunity if you will, quite possibly the chance of a lifetime, the chance to make scientific history, to bring a brand new species to the forefront of the public consciousness."

Will muttered to himself.

"What is it, Mr. Freeman?"

Will shook his head, not willing to further frighten Liz and Zac.

"Mr. Freeman, time is of the essence. Please, if you have something to say, say it."

Will glanced back and couldn't see Liz or Zac standing anywhere nearby.

"We're in danger here and in terrible positioning, to say the least," he said.

Hearing this, Peter approached, gun slung over his shoulder. "Will, what the hell are you talking about?"

Will stood there, silenced for a moment, hesitating before sharing his knowledge.

Will calmly walked up to Chee. "We're being hunted, corralled in here like guinea pigs."

Jonathon, who had been listening, appeared to pale and shrink from cocky and arrogant-assistant, to scared-shitless little school girl at Will's proclamation.

"Once again, Will, what the hell are you talking about?" Peter fired back.

Chee stepped closer to Will and motioned Peter back with his hands. "Mr. Miles, let him speak."

Chapter Thirty-Three

The creatures moved rapidly, as they carried the lifeless body parts of the mangled polar bear in their mouths. The largest parts were carried by the adults, as they galloped over the wide open terrain. One of the youngsters had the decapitated head of the bear firmly secured in its mouth. The group quickly disappeared again into the veil of fog.

Chapter Thirty-Four

"We're being hunted," Will repeated.

Peter had heard enough and approached Will. "Can I have a word with you in private?"

Chee didn't say anything, as the two men moved some distance away.

When they were a safe distance away and secrecy was ensured, Peter turned around. "Look, I don't know what you're trying to pull here, but I suggest you cut it out."

Will appeared perplexed.

"Listen to me. Whatever it is you're out here for, he is not!" Peter said, pointing in the direction of Chee. "Take a look around. It never was about the research. You're being offered a substantial amount of money. My suggestion is to take the money, keep your mouth shut, and do as you're told."

With that, Peter turned his back on Will and walked back to the others, refusing to participate further in the conversation. Will didn't bother to say a word, but followed closely behind Peter. Yet, even if words had come to his mouth, he wouldn't have had the slightest clue how to go about talking to his once, good friend.

I'm not going to get into a peeing contest with a skunk, because you'll lose every time, Will thought to himself.

As the men walked back in silence, he found it hard to believe they were ever even friends in the first place, let alone good friends. Hour by hour, minute by minute, second by second, Peter Miles was resembling no friend that Will Freeman had ever wished to know.

Chapter Thirty-Five

"Mr. Miles?" Chee asked.

Peter walked straight past Chee toward the supplies and equipment. "All taken care of, nothing to worry about."

Will didn't bother making eye contact with Chee as he followed behind Peter. He awkwardly stood there, not knowing whether to help Peter round up the equipment or make small talk. *Hard to imagine we used to be friends. I don't even know you anymore.*

Thankfully, Peter put an end to the silence.

"Will, your people are over there. You know what needs to be done. Now go to it."

With that Will made his way over to where Zac and Liz were waiting.

"We're ready!" Zac shouted, as he saw Will make his way out of the fog that was swirling about. "What the hell took you so long? Liz and I were almost about to play strip poker."

Liz fired Zac a very displeased look and summarily dismissed him. This had no effect on the boldness and cockiness that made up the nature of his character.

"Meeting," Will said, as the look on his face showed his frustration. "Let's get this shit over with. Let's go to it."

Zac cracked a smile, never having heard Will usher as much as a minor cuss in his entire life. *What's gotten into him?*

They worked in silence for several uninterrupted moments, making quick work of getting the food, water, and rest of the supplies ready in a rapid and efficient manner. When they finished what was deemed necessary for their journey to the northwest cliff, each looked at the other with both fear and uncertainty.

Chapter Thirty-Six

The bleak whiteout conditions lifted for a few brief minutes to let the sun peak its head out and illuminate the ice shelf. The sun's life-giving rays almost symbolically blazed the way, as the snowmobiles raced along, and zigzagging in and out toward their intended destination.

For the first time, the beauty of the icy landscape was revealed. It was, almost as if the sun was melting away the mystery and secrets. It was showing off in all its glory.

The sun's rays were contagious, energizing Zac, Will, and Liz. They gained some much needed motivation and vigor as the snowmobiles continued to tear across the landscape. As the wind raced through Will's hair, mixed feelings and uncertainty coursed through him. What was he doing out here? He remained confused about the entire situation.

His mind was racing back and forth, considering every imaginable scenario, and outcome.

What am I doing out here? We're in serious trouble. For crying out loud, snap out of it. We're being hunted.

Chapter Thirty-Seven

"Mr. Miles," Chee said, "Mr. Freeman mentioned that we are being hunted. Do you find this to be true? Is there any evidence to support this notion?"

Peter's shotgun was still slung over his shoulder, as he calmly turned his attention from the surrounding landscape to face Chee. "What do you think?"

Chee lowered his head and approached Peter, slowly, deliberately, and with an aspect of extreme seriousness.

The blow from Chee's right hand, slapping him across the face caught Peter off guard, causing him to stumble backward several steps. "I do not pay you for you to question me. I pay you to think. I pay you to deliver this animal, or animals to me!" Chee said as the tone of his voice rose significantly.

"I am going to ask you one more time. Is Mr. Freeman correct in believing that we are being herded into a position advantageous to the animals?"

Peter looked down at the ice and could see several droplets of blood. He touched his lip with his finger and could see that he was bleeding.

"Mr. Miles!"

Peter looked up, staring at him. "Yes."

Chee scanned the landscape with a serious look. "Interesting."

Chapter Thirty-Eight

Ahead of the three crew members stood the massive, one hundred fifty foot, vertical ice cliff, its walls harboring the ancient mysteries of years gone by. They gazed at it in awe, for several minutes, feeling quite small in the presence of something so massively beautiful.

Will wondered about the age of the ice before him. These types of questions had always seemed to fascinate him. Though not a geologist, hydrologist, nor a glaciologist, he had always harbored a deep respect and admiration for what these sciences examined.

Every part of the earth has a story, he thought to himself. *I wonder what this cliff's story is.*

At the base a constant flow of ice melt ran off from the giant hunk of ice. As the crew approached, the brightly colored walls gave off a hint of blue, a natural, frozen phenomenon.

Will shielded his eyes as the glare from the sun bounced off the wall of ice.

"Here," Liz said, handing him an extra set of her oversized dark glasses.

Will looked down at them in his hand and then up toward Liz. As he put them on, she couldn't help but laugh.

"Great," Zac said, "you're bringing the 1950s out here to the arctic. Does Marylyn Monroe know you stole her glasses?"

"Don't listen to him," Liz said, "you look great."

Zac rolled his eyes, holding his tongue, fighting back the urge to make a sarcastic joke, but he didn't.

Liz looked around nervously, scanning the cliff for areas in which an animal could hide or conceal itself. "You don't see any of those tracks around here, do you?"

Will shook his head. "Nothing since we passed the other tracks. I've been watching. Trust me."

The steepness of the cliff seized him, as he looked toward the top of the ice cliff. "I can't do this," he said, taking a few steps back.

Zac put his arm around his good buddy and smiled. "The trick is not to fall, big guy."

Zac took a few steps away back so he could get a good perspective on the cliff. "If this wasn't ice, I could skitter up this thing in no time, with no ropes, or assistance, I might add."

Will stood there with his arms crossed and a rather sickened look on his face. "I know, but I'm not you. I'm not a rock climber. You know that I would never try and tackle something like this, never mind the fact that it's made of ice."

"That's the fun part," Zac said, "one slip and you're gone. It makes every move potentially your last."

Liz fired Zac a mean glare. "Enough, okay."

Will shook his head.

Liz had come over and put her hand on his shoulder. "We're going to get you through this, but more importantly, we're all going to get through this together."

Her tone alone was reassuring to him, and he wanted to tell her how much he already appreciated the tone and nature of her caring, but he said nothing. He stood there silent, staring, wondering, pondering, how in the world he was going to make it safely to the top.

His mind raced thinking of everyone who had ever insulted him, doubted him, blown him off, or believed the business model that was his life, would ever work. Time after time people told him that he couldn't be the nice guy and ascend to the top, that he needed to change his ways and be a meaner, cockier version of himself. He knew that this was his chance staring him straight in the face, to silence all the critics, to destroy the demons that had haunted him for far too long.

He looked up at the ice cliff one more time. *This cliff has to be conquered. I must do this.*

Chapter Thirty-Nine

The pockets of fog continued to roll in across the white terrain as the creatures sprinted at top speed, galloping as fast as they could toward their intended destination. Bringing up the rear were two massive adults. In the middle of the herd, were the guarded and protected juveniles, the adults offering them protection from any would-be predators lurking nearby.

The group continued at a high pace, pounding across their white environment, blending in beautifully with the white, pristine habitat. Their sheer mass alone caused the ground to rumble and shake.

The group continued to move in perfect harmony with each other, completely in tune with the dominant male leading the pack. They banked hard right, around a set of freshly laid snowmobile tracks, turning on a dime, just as modern day birds fly in unison. Everything was efficient, deliberate, and at a high pace.

Onward they pounded across the terrain, and then in an instant they stopped. The dominant male came to an abrupt halt and paced in a tight circle around a set of freshly laid human tracks.

A chorus of excited shrieks came from the group. The peace was shattered with all kinds of terrifying snarls and yelps. Individuals pounded on their chests, let out ungodly sounds, and beat the ice with their powerful arms.

The tracks led toward the base of the ice cliff.

Chapter Forty

Will tilted his head up at the wall, got dizzy, and stumbled backward a few steps. *I can do this. I can climb that. You're gonna do this, Will.*

Zac patted him on the shoulder. "Quit talking to yourself."

Will looked surprised. "I didn't say anything."

Zac smiled, patting his good friend on the back once more. "I can hear your thoughts, bro. Plus, I know you like I know myself. Don't sweat it."

Will smiled at him. "I'm good. I feel good."

Zac nodded back. *Easy to say when you're on the ground.*

The ice cliff towered above them, as a light snow began to fall and pockets of fog began moving in. It was clear to all that they needed to get moving, and quickly.

"Throw me that rope!" Liz shouted to Will. Apparently, again frozen with fear, he was eventually able to throw her the rope.

"Thanks!" she shouted back.

Liz looked back over at Will who continued to be wrestling with the idea of climbing the ice cliff.

"You can do it," she said.

He looked over at her, "you're that confident in me?"

She continued to tighten her harness around her and fastened it, and then double and triple checked herself. "Yes, I am."

She made her way over to him and his pulse began to quicken slightly. Their eyes met, as they stood about a foot apart.

"Will, you're going to make it to the top, just like you're going to make it in life. I'll personally see to it."

For a brief second he had forgotten about everything, his career, wife, dilemmas, financial problems, expedition and just about everything else. Her eyes were arguably the most beautiful he had ever seen. They were a lovely hazel color.

"Hey!" a voice shouted from nearby, startling both of them.

Zac stood there with arms folded, shaking his head. "This is a family rated place!"

Chapter Forty-One

The dominant male pounded its two powerful arms down on to the ice, causing the ice to fracture and splinter under the immense weight and power of the animal.

This was followed by a cacophony of sounds and shrieks as the area was bristling with creatures pounding and pacing back and forth, like caged lions in a zoo. They each showed and tried to assert their dominance over the others.

Nothing in this world could match them.

Chapter Forty-Two

As Liz, Will, and Zac prepared for their ascent to the top of the ice cliff, the other part of the crew was hard at work searching the flat and wide-open terrain. The area they were searching was vast, hampered by crevasses, challenging weather, predators, and an unknown species whose footprints kept popping up everywhere.

The crew kept spotting footprints around them as if they were being corralled by an invisible perimeter. Wherever they went, the footprints were there, as if the creatures were watching them, waiting for the crew to cross the boundaries.

Chee approached Jonathon who was busy loading both of their day backpacks. "Did you make the arrangements we discussed back on campus?"

Jonathon instantly dropped both bags, like an attentive dog, loyal as ever to his master. "Yes, sir."

"No mistakes," Chee replied, walking away with his hands behind his back.

Jonathon stopped for a moment, itching to know, "but what if we don't find anything?"

Chee paused, with his back to Jonathon, still keeping his hands clasped behind his back. He then turned to face his assistant and in his usual tone addressed him. "We will find it. It is out there. Have no doubt, we will find it indeed."

Chee walked away. As it appeared, Peter had been listening. He had been listening the entire time while double and triple checking that he had the necessary amounts of ammo and firearms to tackle such beasts.

Jonathon gave Peter a snide look, as he was in no mood to deal with the likes of him. "Mind your own business. Go back to your weapons. That's all you are hired for, the only reason in hell why you're even here. You're just a gun."

The comment took Peter completely by surprise. "Excuse me?"

Before Jonathon could even respond, he was staring down the barrel of Peter's shotgun. The weapon was pointed squarely at his forehead. Jonathan's pulse quickened and beads of sweat began rolling down his face.

"Now you listen to me, you little shit disturber," Peter forcefully said through clenched teeth, jamming the shotgun tighter against Jonathon's forehead. "I've had enough of your shit!"

He grabbed the back of Jonathon's head, forcing and jamming it even tighter against the barrel of the gun. He struggled, but he was no match against Peter's strength.

"One more word and you'll be a permanent resident."

With that, he released Jonathon who stumbled backward hunched over and gasping for air.

Chapter Forty-Three

"You're doing great!" Liz shouted down to Will, as they were almost halfway to the top of the ice cliff.

Will didn't reply, but gave her a thumbs up.

The ice cliff was the most intimidating wall he had ever seen in his life. Even as a child, on trips to Yosemite National Park, he would never approach the base of mountains, the sheer act of looking straight up the rock wall sent chills up his spine and made him dizzy.

On the other hand, Zac was a seasoned pro at such endeavors. He saw the cliff for what it really was, a jagged, easy to ascend, rock wall. The wall jutted in and out with parts projecting out and others receding, thereby not allowing a straight shot to the top. He found it rather easy.

Will rested for a moment, pondering his current plight. *What the hell am I doing up here?*

Zac wiped beads of sweat from his forehead and gazed out over the open terrain, stunned to find that he could actually see very little.

They had all been so intent on having a successful climb to the top that they didn't realize the fog that had moved into the area in dense pockets. Zac could see the landscape about a mile out, but directly beneath him had turned into a complete white-out. They couldn't see the ice from whence they came, adding to the eerie-ness of hanging off the edge of the ice cliff.

"You're doing great!" Zac shouted up to Will. "Just keep going and don't look down!"

As the three of them slowly began moving again, a strange sensation began to ripple through their bodies.

"Hey, hey, hey. What the hell's goin' on?" Zac yelled.

The rope that connected all three of them had begun to violently ripple, and then the unthinkable happened; it began to swing rapidly back and forth. All three whipped back and forth, their bodies crashing and slamming into the side of the ice cliff.

"What's happening?" Liz screamed, trying to grip something with her hands. The three of them continued their terrifying fight to hang on and there was nothing on the wall to grasp.

"Just hold on!" Will shouted, "hold on!"

Zac craned his head downward in a desperate attempt to get a fix on what was causing this, but it was no use as the area below was still shrouded in fog. The three were completely helpless. They were repeatedly thrown from side to side and smashed violently into the ice.

The movement suddenly stopped, leaving them only swaying gently back and forth, to the end of their rollercoaster ordeal. All three of them dangled with tight and tense bodies, refusing to let go of their death grips on the rope. Everything was eerily quiet, as they held on in silence. The fog smothered all sight and sound.

Chapter Forty-Four

The ice vehicle wasn't making very good headway. Peter piloted the hi-tech machine with Jonathon seated in the passenger seat next to him. Chee was comfortably observing the landscape from the back. The vehicle continued onward through the bleak and blustery conditions. Visibility wasn't good, but every now and then they entered small patches where they could see.

"Anything, Mr. Miles?" Chee asked, continuing to look out the side window.

"No," Peter replied. "Right now our priority is getting out of this fog bank safely. We can't see a damn thing. That's why we're taking it slowly."

Jonathon pressed his head against the glass and muttered to himself. "Slower than hell."

"What was that?" Peter demanded, slamming the vehicle into park. "What did you say?"

Jonathon stared straight ahead into the fog bank. "Do you really think we're going to find what we're looking for going zero miles per hour?"

Peter fiercely gripped the wheel and looked out over his left shoulder, hoping desperately for better visibility in the white out. It was no use, as the fog was socked in, and they couldn't see a thing. It was as if they were floating in a completely white void, with no depth perception. All senses useless except for hearing.

Peter instinctively rolled the window down, listening closely for what his surroundings might tell him. Nothing. Only the occasional creaking of the ice greeted his eardrums.

"Didn't think you had the skills to navigate through something like this," Jonathan muttered.

Peter smiled while resting his hands atop the steering wheel, taking in the entire scene consisting of fog and more fog. Jonathon was caught completely off guard, as Peter's right fist slammed his head into the passenger side window. He hit the window hard.

Dazed by the blow and confused, Jonathon instinctively made an attempt to lunge at Peter. Yet before he could even move a few inches, Peter's right hand had him pinned up against the window. "You're not going to say another word!"

Before Peter could say more, Chee calmly intervened from the back seat. "Gentlemen, enough."

Peter slowly retracted his hand, as Jonathon rubbed his jaw and neck.

"Both of you gentlemen are going to have to find a way to deal with one another. I will not have you ruining my plans. There is far too much at stake here. Is this understood?" Chee looked over at Peter first.

"Yes," Peter replied.

Chee then turned to Jonathon who was still rubbing his jaw. "And you?"

"Yes, sir," Jonathon replied, like a child who had just been scolded by his father.

"Now, Mr. Miles, can we drive?"

Peter was staring intensely at something that had caught his attention out in the fog bank.

"Mr. Miles?" Chee repeated.

Peter motioned for everyone to be quiet and all conversation stopped. Patience paid off, as a mysterious shape was coming into view. Something was out there.

Chapter Forty-Five

No one spoke, or barely breathed, as all three were extremely shaken by what had just happened.

Even Zac, the grandmaster of adventure, was visibly rattled as he took several long, deep breaths. "Dude, is everyone okay up there?"

Will surprisingly found himself able to answer, "yes."

"Think so," Liz said from above.

Will was just about to reposition himself when the rope once again began to sway back and forth. The three were helpless, as they began to clamor for stability, but there was none to be found.

Back and forth the group was battered against the wall of ice, their bodies thrown like ragdolls. They were rendered completely helpless.

"The pick," Liz gasped, her hand just missing it by inches as she swung by.

Her eyes focused on the ice pick shoved into the ice several inches below, just out of her reach. As the rope swung by the ice pick one more time, she measured her arm reach and plotted her moves. With all her might, she extended her arm as far as she could, catching the very end of the ice pick handle. The impact caused the ice pick to break free, but it wasn't in Liz's hand, and it began to fall.

"Watch out!" she screamed.

But it was no use. Amidst all the chaos and yelling, neither Will nor Zac heard the warning.

The ice pick went plummeting down, narrowly missing Will's head. Unfortunately for Zac, he wasn't so lucky. He never knew what hit him, and was instantly knocked unconscious, as the ice pick struck him on the forehead. As his body slumped over, the rope continued to swing back and forth. Neither Will nor Liz were aware that their friend was losing copious amounts of blood and was dangling, unconscious.

Chapter Forty-Six

The dominant male suddenly moved away from the rope, something else catching his attention. Visibility was still minimal at best, and the base of the ice cliff remained mired in white fog. The creature, however, could hear very well and bolted away on four legs, making his way out toward the ice field, to join the others in their chorus of disturbing cries and shrieks.

The thick fog remained, visually isolating the humans from the creatures. The giant tracks remained also, and led away from the cliff and out on to the field of ice.

Chapter Forty-Seven

The dense fog had separated just enough for the crew to have a look through its veil of secrecy.

"Mr. Miles," Chee whispered, "start the vehicle and inch forward ever so slightly."

Peter did as he was told, the lights of the ice vehicle barely penetrating the white void ahead of them.

"Easy now," Chee said while the ice vehicle crept forward.

Slowly the vehicle crept across the ice at no faster than five miles per hour. As they neared the object that had caught their attention, Chee motioned for Peter to bring the vehicle to a halt and cut the lights.

Peter slowed the vehicle and quietly put it into park. Lying before them were the fresh remains of a once large, polar bear carcass, that had been ravaged by something or somethings.

No one said a word for several seconds as they all stared at the dead animal, each silently formulating many questions. *Had this most magnificent of beasts been brought down by natural causes, or had something physically taken it down,* Peter thought to himself.

"Gentlemen," Chee said, breaking the silence, "what are we waiting for?"

Jonathon and Peter simultaneously opened their doors, careful not to close them too loudly. Peter was first on the scene and knelt down next to the animal. "This is fresh."

Chee stood some several feet behind him and instantly saw that the head of the polar bear had been severely damaged. He pointed with his cane toward the skull of the animal. Peter instantly took in the damage at which Chee was pointing.

The head of the animal was completely smashed and sunken into the ice. Its form and shape were gone, as the bone structure on the side of the skull facing upward had been obliterated.

Peter slightly nudged the head with the end of his rifle. "Whatever did this, delivered an absolutely fatal blow to this animal. It most likely didn't even know what struck it."

Chee continued to hover, his eyes glistening with anticipation. "I think we both know what could have done this."

Peter leaned over to better view his way up and down the torso of the mangled polar bear. All of a sudden he stood up straight and turned around. His attention had been diverted.

"What is it, Mr. Miles?"

"Where's that assistant of yours?"

Chee didn't even bat an eye at the question. "Please focus, Mr. Miles. Nature is telling us something here. We must be as alert as possible and as in tune with our surroundings as we can."

Chapter Forty-Eight

Will, now able to think more calmly, wondered why Zac had not been making any sarcastic quips about their ordeal. Finally, able to untangle the rope enough to be able to look down, he saw Zac, dangling, lifeless at the bottom of the rope.

"Zac!" he screamed, his voice breaking Liz out of her daze. She came back to her senses, staring down at him. "What's wrong?"

He could barely mumble the words out of his mouth. The shock of the moment coupled with the fact that they were perched precariously on the side of an ice cliff didn't make things any better.

"Oh my God!" Liz screamed, "hold on, Will, we need to help him!"

Liz tried to gather herself for a moment, to make sure her mind and body were in sync before she unhooked herself from the rope and began to descend toward Will. Her years of rock climbing paid off with as much cool and collected confidence as could be expected under the circumstances.

"What happened? Did you see anything?" she said as she had reached Will's level.

"Didn't see anything," he said, while taking another quick glance at Zac, "we need to act fast."

"Right," she said, "we need to get him down quickly as possible so I can have a look."

Will was hit with overwhelming dreadful questions. What had just happened? More importantly, who or what in the world had shaken their rope and almost literally shaken all of them off the side of the cliff?

Chapter Forty-Nine

Jonathon fumbled with his zipper and finally managed to button his pants. He had been needing to go pee for what seemed like an eternity. As Chee and Peter were examining the dead polar bear, he had made the decision to slip away, unnoticed, to relieve himself.

His fingers had lost their dexterity due to the cold. *Damn, it's cold. Just think happy thoughts, like the beaches of the Caribbean, and all the money from this godforsaken trip, in an offshore bank account somewhere.* He smiled to himself for a second, pausing to fully take in his daydream.

He had only been gone a few minutes, but the conditions had seemed to significantly worsen. *I think it's that way back,* he thought to himself.

He set out toward where he believed Chee and Peter would be, analyzing the remains of a polar bear and conversing over the possibility of a mythical creature that he didn't believe existed.

How could such a creature exist, in the technological age in which we live, he thought to himself.

After what he reckoned to be several hundred steps of walking into the fog, he was dumbfounded to have not stumbled upon the men. *Where are they?* Jonathon had what most people considered to be a photographic memory, and would have bet his last dime that the vision of Chee and Peter hunched over the carcass of a dead animal would have popped into view by now, but it had not.

"Now what?" he mumbled to himself.

The fog appeared to be worse. He held his hand up to his face, barely able to see his fingertips. Visibility was a maximum of a foot at best.

Now what?

He was disoriented and had no idea from which direction he had come. He did the only logical thing that came to his mind.

"Help!" he shouted for as long as his vocal chords and lungs held out.

After a while Jonathon paused, and became as still and as quiet as his partially numb body would allow.

"Dammit!" he cursed aloud, kicking at the ice.

His mind instantly began unraveling with different scenarios of how he would die way out here in the middle of nowhere. He would starve and wither away to nothing. Or, all the creatures in the area would surely be aware of his presence, and he would suffer a terrible fate at their hands.

Jonathon's hair suddenly stood on end, as a growl came from out of the fog.

Shit!

Chapter Fifty

Will took one quick glance below at the base of the ice cliff. He could see nothing but a thick layer of fog hugging the ice, blocking their vision.

Liz scanned below and then back to Zac, who was still apparently lifeless. "Whatever was down there seems to be gone. We need to get down quickly. He can't wait much longer."

"Let's get to it," Will replied, looking down at his good buddy, just dangling there.

Liz repositioned herself, making sure that she had a firm, correct grip on the rope. "Now we're going to do this together, okay?"

"Damn straight." His response startled her, and she smiled at him. Then the seriousness of their task hit them like a ton of bricks.

"We're going to have to carry him down," Liz ordered Will.

Will was so completely in tune with the task at hand that he had, at least for the moment, forgotten the fear that had previously paralyzed him. His fear was real. Zac's injury was real. The threat at the base of the ice cliff was real, but for the first time in his entire life, the confidence flowing through his veins, was the most real and pure feeling he had ever experienced.

Chapter Fifty-One

What the hell was that? Jonathon thought to himself, the sound of a vicious growl coming from somewhere inside the thick veil of fog. The sound happened again, and this time it was closer. Jonathon instinctively fumbled for his phone.

It was too late. The sleek and stealthy predator had emerged from the whiteness. Before Jonathon, stood an adult male wolf, its jaw agape, as it growled a low rumble.

Naturally, Jonathon's first urge was to turn and run, but he fought that off and stood his ground. With his heart in his mouth, he stood firmly in place, as the wolf inched closer toward him.

He was surprised at the timidness of the animal, expecting the creature to lunge at him and tear his throat out, but it did not.

To his relief, the wolf took one last look at him, and darted off into the fog.

"That's right, bitch, run home to Mommy!"

No sooner had he said that, when something else caught his attention. It was moving fast. An ungodly cry came from something within the fog. Jonathon weakly stepped forward.

"Here, wolfie, come back. Here wolfie," he whispered, reaching out into the unknown white, as he stumbled hesitantly forward.

Chapter Fifty-Two

Peter's head instantly shot up, feeling the presence of something or things close by.

"What is it, Mr. Miles?"

Peter raised his hand to signal for silence. "I don't know."

The two stood there, completely shrouded in silence and fog. Chee pointed toward the ice vehicle.

"Right," Peter whispered, rising to his feet and began sprinting toward the ice vehicle with Chee close behind.

Sounds and noises of all sorts began building around them. They continued their seemingly endless rush toward the safety of the vehicle. Peter was first to reach it as his outstretched hand literally smashed into the driver's side door. He quickly opened the door, and climbed inside. Leaning over, he managed to creak open the passenger side door for Chee.

Something was wrong. He fired up the vehicle, the headlights glaring out into the white. Chee hadn't appeared.

Peter sat there with his hands tightly gripped around the steering wheel, waiting for Chee to jump into the vehicle at any moment, allowing them to make their getaway.

"Com' on, com' on!"

Peter left the vehicle running, grabbed the shotgun as he opened the door and jumped out. He fired off several rounds into the air and then took a calculated risk, and unloaded several more rounds on to the path over which he had just run. He paid little attention to the fact that Chee was still somewhere out there. He continued to fire several more shots, aiming at the sounds that were now everywhere.

The Chancellor then miraculously emerged from the fog, and motioned Peter to get inside the vehicle. No sooner had they raced inside the vehicle, when an enormous boom came down on top of it, causing the roof to partially cave in.

"Drive, Mr. Miles. Drive!"

The vehicle moved forward as images, clear and blurry, were now on all sides.

"Faster, Mr. Miles., faster!"

Peter pressed down harder on the gas, as the vehicle sped ahead into the unknown.

"Mr. Miles!" Chee shouted, when an enormous, white, shaggy arm came into view and smashed through the windshield, sending shards of glass in all directions. The cold air rushed in, chilling them further.

Peter instinctively swerved the vehicle, just in time to avoid another arm swinging toward them. The vehicle raced off into the unknown. The creatures followed in close pursuit, galloping on all fours, like modern day silverback gorillas, hell bent on their prey.

Chapter Fifty-Three

Will and Liz shared a quick glance. "Whatever it was," she said, "we have no choice but to head down. We'll figure it out and make sure Zac's safe."

They acted quickly and efficiently, reaching Zac who was still alive, but dangling unconscious, on his rope. Zac's head was now encrusted with dried blood. He also appeared to have been badly battered by the repeated slamming into the ice wall.

Liz and Will worked to firmly secure themselves to each other, and Zac to their backs so that they could move him down to the ice. The goal was plain and simple, to rappel down, with Zac strapped to them, until they reached the bottom.

"You ready?" Liz asked, "we can do this. We'll be down in no time."

"I've imagined doing something like this my whole life, but never had the guts before." Will confessed.

Liz smiled. "Now's your chance, here we go."

And with that they sent themselves, shooting, in tandem, away from the wall of ice as they pushed off with their feet. Zac remained unconscious and snugly strapped to them. They bounced back to the wall and repeated over and over until they were halfway down the ice cliff.

"We're doing good!" Will shouted, as they once again flew out and away from the wall.

"Just keep it up!" Liz shot back.

They paused on the wall after several intense minutes of rappelling. Suddenly, everything began to shake violently again.

They both looked down toward the base of the ice wall but could see nothing.

"Will, do something!"

Will did the only thing he could think of, and reached into his pack, pulling out a bright red flare. Managing to successfully light the flare on the first try, he dropped it toward the foggy bottom, the bright streak of light piercing and shooting out its glow as it continued its plummet.

They hung, suspended in silence for a moment, their eyes still straining toward the base, waiting to see what would happen next. After several terrifying long, quiet, seconds, the rope began to shake once more, and they began to sway back and forth.

"Will!" Liz shouted, her voice wavered in terror.

He reached again, but missed his pack. The jolt of the rope flew back and forth throwing him off balance.

"Try again!" Liz shouted, as they continued their wild swinging, back and forth.

Finally, Will managed to grab another precious flare. He bit down tightly around it, and for a split second feared that he might actually have bitten right through it.

The flare made a sizzling sound as it was successfully lit. Will took one look down and dropped it precisely on what he believed to be his intended target. The rope instantly stopped moving. They looked at each other, and Will stressed, "we need to get down, quickly."

He scanned the rope above for possible fracture or damage. When all seemed okay, or at least as good as it could possibly be, they continued their descent.

At long last, their feet touched down on the ice at the base. They were elated to have made it even though their bodies were battered and legs were burning with exertion. Still, one thing remained certain. They couldn't see a damn thing.

Chapter Fifty-Four

The menacing sound that came from inside the veil of thick, white fog stopped Jonathon dead in his tracks, but his trembling hands kept searching, as if reaching out for some form of miraculous help. However, none was to be found in this frigid and unforgiving land.

"Help!" he cried out, again and again, setting his lungs on fire with the volume of his cries.

His desperate pleas were answered with unmistakable growls. He fell to his knees, as if pleading with the being that was keeping him captive in this white abyss.

"God, please help me," he cried out as his body began to shiver and tremble.

The galloping that, at first, only appeared to his left now surrounded him. There were sounds of growling and snarling on all sides.

Defiantly, he stood up again to face whatever it was that was within the blanket of fog. His body began to tremble more and more, as if he no longer had control of his muscles. Every part of him shook uncontrollably. His heart pounded madly, feeling as though it would explode from his chest.

As he made the sign of the cross, an enormous, white, shaggy arm emerged from the fog, ripping him from his last stand. His screams were the most horrific one could imagine.

Chapter Fifty-Five

"Mr. Miles!" Chee shouted, as the front of the ice vehicle slammed into a crevasse that neither of them had seen.

"Dammit!" Peter cursed, as the front of the ice vehicle hung partially in the crevasse.

"Can we reverse?" Chee asked, as both of them were thrown forward but remained hanging by their seatbelts.

The front of the ice vehicle was jammed down into the crevasse at a thirty-five degree angle. The backend was still up on the ice. Peter carefully unbuckled his seatbelt and advised Chee to stay still.

He did his best to squeeze his hand into the back seat and reach for his backpack. *I need my flashlight.* His right hand managed to reach his flashlight, and he fumbled with it for several seconds before managing to turn it on. The bright light illuminated the partial darkness that they were in.

"Mr. Miles, shine it down there."

Peter turned the flashlight around and shone it through where the windshield had been. They sat in stunned silence at what lay before them. They were looking several hundred feet down to the bottom of an icy abyss.

"Mr. Miles, shine the light over there."

Peter slowly moved the light up from the bottom to about halfway up one of the walls to reveal what appeared to be a massive cave system.

"Right there. Stop!" Chee breathed.

Peter moved the light back and forth, slowly, over what appeared to be an opening halfway up the cave wall.

"What is that?" Peter asked.

"Mr. Miles, the creature that attacked us is not alone."

Chapter Fifty-Six

"Right here!" Liz shouted, "here on top of the blanket."

Will came trotting over as fast as he could muster; Zac still slumped over his shoulders, substantially weighing him down. He carefully placed his friend down on top of the blanket.

"Hand me that," Liz said.

Will reached for a bandanna that was in her backpack.

"We need to clean this wound," she said while dipping the edge of the bandanna into a small container of alcohol.

She dabbed the bandanna around the open wound. She directed Will to look for something clean to use as a bandage.

"Easy, woman," Zac said groggily, as his eyes opened slowly, just like out of a Hollywood script.

"Zac!" Will called, running over and bending over toward his friend, "how do you feel?"

"Like shit, but sure as hell beats being dead."

Will reached forward and gave him a big bear hug.

"Easy man, I'm wounded, not dead."

"Sorry. I thought the worst."

Liz knelt down to look at the wound. "How you feeling?"

Zac looked at her with the cocky ass smile that had typified his personality for so long. "Has the money been direct deposited into our accounts yet?"

Will shook his head, but with a smile on his face. "At least we know you're okay."

Suddenly, the climbing rope was yanked away by something that instantly raced away from them.

"Hey!" Will shouted, at the top of his lungs, as he chased after the rope that disappeared into the fog.

"Will!" Liz shouted, as she threw him a flare.

As Will ran off shouting and waving his arms frantically in the air, Zac tried to stand.

"You stay put," Liz commanded, as she ran off after Will.

"Hey, stop!" Will shouted, as he continued to run through pockets of dense fog, half expecting that any second he would plunge to his death into one of the crevasses.

On and on he ran until he stopped, his senses indicating the presence of something. He knew he wasn't alone. A sharp wind cut right through the area, chilling him to the bone for a brief second. It blew away the surrounding fog and revealed the backside of something massive.

At first he wasn't quite sure what he was seeing. It moved, causing him to almost jump out of his skin.

The massive head of the creature turned, revealing razor-sharp teeth that thrust out both sides of its mouth. Its smashed-in nose gave it a most gruesome, hideous appearance.

There it is. Will was paralyzed, incapable of screaming or moving. He was completely at the mercy of the gigantic beast that stood before him.

For a brief second, he felt as if he were one of the great explorers of the past who stumbled on the legendary Sasquatch. However, he was no explorer, and this was no legendary creature of myth and folklore. This, was very possibly, the last thing Will would see before dying.

The hideous beast peered down at him as it snarled, emphasizing the razor sharp teeth that lined its mouth, making Will feel puny and insignificant in the face of something so huge. He could hear footsteps behind him, but his eyes remained fixed on the creature. He hoped like hell that it was Liz behind him.

The creature took one last look at him and then charged off in to the fog, with their rope in hand. Liz saw the tail end of it as she neared and screamed a shriek of utter terror as she witnessed the thing bolting away on all fours.

Chapter Fifty-Seven

Where am I, Jonathon thought to himself, as his body had a strange, eerie, light feeling to it. It was as if he was floating above the ice, soaring over large patches in a matter of seconds.

He was tightly clutched in the hand of one of the creatures as it made its way across the ice on its other three legs. The pain rushed all the way to his head. For what seemed like hours, he felt like his head would explode from the extreme pressure the animal's grip was having on him.

Another of the creatures, galloping alongside, took several lunges at him. The creature's mouth came ever so close to ripping Jonathon from his captor's grip. His captor changed direction to protect his meal from the freeloaders that were desperately trying to rip the body away.

Creatures were emerging from everywhere as Jonathon's beast continued to gallop ahead, with his human captive squeezed in his right hand. Horrific sounds from everywhere could be heard, as if the entire area was now awakening to the fact that fresh meat was on the horizon.

Jonathon was now near the point of unconsciousness, his body crushed inside the animal's fearsome, vice-like grip. He was suspended upside down and could see creatures of all shapes and sizes in fast pursuit. He saw that everything was now converging upon them.

Then all of the sudden, like a mother dropping a newborn baby, Jonathon's body was released. The pain was incredible, as he hit hard, sending flashes of pain every which way through his body. He had been dropped from some ten feet above the ice.

Pain flashed everywhere in his body, as he managed to somehow roll over onto his back. Lifting his head up with every last inch of strength he could muster, he was now able to see that creatures of all shapes and sizes had formed a large circle around him and his captor.

He stared at the foot of the creature, still stunned by the sheer size of the animal. It roared at the other creatures surrounding them, refusing to give up his prize. Several of the creatures lunged hungrily toward Jonathon with their jaws. He felt himself at the point of no return, the point where he could feel his life was about to end.

God please let me die before everything converges on me.

His entire existence began to flash before his weary eyes, and he cursed the day he ever met Chancellor Stephen Chee. The money, the fame, the fortune would be meaningless, as his body would be devoured and ripped apart by the beings that now surrounded him on all sides.

Soon it will be over. Death will come quickly, he thought to himself as he lay on his back, too weak to lift his head anymore to see the scene that was still unfolding.

The creature that had captured him sent both fists plummeting down on the ice in a territorial display, smashing bits and pieces of ice, shaking the ice beneath with its terrifying power. The beast began to pace wildly around Jonathon's near lifeless body, signaling to all that he was the dominant male and this was not only his territory, but, more importantly, his property.

Without warning, a large gap in the tight circle opened, sending two of the massive creatures racing forward and on to the backside of Jonathon's captor. One of the creatures lunged and landed on the back of the gigantic creature, while the other made its way around the front and caught the animal by the face, dragging it down to the ice. The scene resembled that of prehistoric raptors jumping on the backs of their dinosaurian prey as they tugged and slashed at the animal, trying to bring it to its knees.

Jonathon's captor was in serious trouble as it was being pulled down viciously by its face and one of the others began chomping down on his back. The sounds were horrific as the snarling, growling and roaring from within the circle grew and grew. He remained on his back to weak to move. His only view was the pieces of sky above him, as the attack continued.

He gasped, as his view suddenly took in two glowing red eyes. Peering down at him were the blazing red eyes of one of the baby creatures. It stood completely still, looking at the puny human. While Jonathon's captor fell to its knees and the creatures savagely ripped into its body, another set of glowing red eyes emerged and stared down at Jonathon. Before he could even get a sense of what was about to happen, Jonathon was completely surrounded by glowing red eyes peering down at him.

There was no scream, no panic, no last cry for help as everything converged upon his body in the ultimate feeding frenzy.

Chapter Fifty-Eight

Peter stared in stunned silence, as his mind began to slowly process what he was seeing. "Those are dens," he whispered.

"Precisely, Mr. Miles. Now we have evidence that the species is in this region. For so many years I have waited for this moment, and here below lies evidence of a vast community of these animals."

Peter's hearing focused and his pulse raised at the sound of digging and scratching. The creatures were furiously trying to dig around the ice vehicle to extricate it. In a coordinated team effort, they were trying to hoist the vehicle back to the surface as some pulled violently at the back end of it. The ice vehicle was slowly being hauled out of the crevasse.

"They're pulling us up!" Peter shouted.

He reached around to the backseat and grabbed his backpack while the car was slowly being inched out of the darkness and into the light. His hands grasped the rope that would be their only chance for escape.

Chee looked at him with a sense of urgency. "It will have to do."

Peter began tightly securing the rope to the steering wheel of the ice vehicle. He looped the rope in and out several times before finally giving it several firm tugs. Chee then tossed the rope out his passenger side window.

"We will make it," Chee said, sliding through the window and beginning his descent.

Peter watched in silence, as the chancellor slowly made his way down the rope.

What about Will and the others, he thought to himself.

This was his chance to ditch Chee and the expedition that seemed doomed for failure from the start. For a moment he stared off into the darkness of the abyss, letting his mind roam.

The image of all the money that he was still owed being deposited into his off shore bank account came rushing forth, causing him to stare down the rope once more. The vehicle was being pulled out of the crevasse at a much quicker pace now, and Peter quickly slid out the window, beginning his descent into the ice cave.

Chapter Fifty-Nine

"Easy, easy," Will said, as Liz came rushing forth into his arms, "hey, hey, it's okay."

She was visibly shaken by the sight of the gigantic creature galloping away from them. "What was that?"

Will shook his head and stared off into the fog where the creature had just stood.

"Will, answer me, what was that?"

"The claw," he muttered.

"What?"

"The claw! The claw! Chee showed Zac and me a claw of one of these creatures back at the university. I didn't believe it. I thought it was a hoax or something."

Liz stared at him. "What do you think it is?"

Will shook his head. "It's a whole new species. A primate. Ice gorillas."

"So you think these are primates?" she asked.

Will nodded. "The most fearsome kind that has ever existed, by my account, unmatched in the animal world. They're some type of enormous primate. It's possible they migrated up here via some ancient land bridge, thousands, maybe even tens of thousands, of years ago. Eventually, over time they blended into this white environment, becoming the dominant land predator here."

"How'd they get so big?"

"Their food source must be abundant. This place is more fruitful and lush than meets the eye. I'm certain they're tapping into different food sources up here like: polar bears, wolves, seals, and possibly even each other."

Liz looked stunned. "Cannibalism?"

"It's possible. Whatever it takes to survive, the strongest always find a way."

"What's going to happen when the world discovers this species?"

Will paused for a second, and stepped away from Liz as she stood and shivered against the cold wind. "I'm not certain anyone's ever made it out of here alive. For centuries now they may have fiercely protected this place, a refuge if you will for their kind."

Liz turned and looked directly into his eyes. "We need to get out of here."

Will's eyes widened, realizing he had made a grave mistake. "Zac's back there by himself all alone!"

Chapter Sixty

Peter's hands felt as if they were on fire, as he continued his descent. His senses were on heightened alert, as he traveled down and into the depths of the unknown cave.

The light from up above became dimmer and dimmer.

"Mr. Miles, I am almost down!" Chee shouted from below, his voice echoing off the walls of the cave.

"Hang tight, I'm almost there, too."

Peter stopped for a moment and hung suspended in the darkness. Above him he could see the light from either side of the ice vehicle. The strange thing was that the rope he was hanging on was no longer being lifted upward by the creatures trying to excavate the vehicle from the crevasse.

He would almost rather have had the creatures scratching and clawing around above, to give him a sense of where they were. Now, as he was about to enter what appeared to be their lair, he had a very uneasy feeling in his stomach.

He continued on down, sensing that the bottom was close. He was anxious for his feet to touch down on terra firma. At long last his feet hit solid ice, and then he wasn't quite sure if that was a good or a bad thing. He had a sick feeling, and uneasiness that was growing in his gut.

Standing tall at the bottom of the ice cave, he couldn't see a thing, and realized Chee had swiped the flashlight from him. *Son of a bitch. It's dark here.*

It was completely, pitch black, and, as he extended his hand directly in front of his face, he could see nothing.

Peter crept forward, afraid to take big steps for fear of the unknown. *This is useless.*

He stood there in complete silence, wondering what to do next. *And to where in the hell did Chee disappear?*

Chapter Sixty-One

Will and Liz ran as fast as they could without stumbling. In and out of pockets of fog they ran as they feared for Zac, but their brains couldn't get over the creature they had both witnessed.

They ran onward, and Will's heartbeat increased rapidly when he saw Zac slumped over with his head down. *Is he....*

Liz was first to get to Zac and bent down instantly to check his pulse. Will could see her bent down next to Zac, but he was still some distance away, unable to determine what was happening. *If anything has happened to him, I'll never forgive myself for leaving him.*

As Will drew closer he could now see that Liz was smiling, and Zac was sitting up straight.

"Seems our friend here decided to take a quick nap right out here in the open," she said as she stood up and brushed herself off.

Will bent down to Zac's level. "Asshole!"

Liz bent down once again and brushed her hand ever so slightly to his forehead where the ice pick had slammed into his head. "Amazing that you're okay. It was way too much of a close call."

Zac was touched by the comment, shocked that Liz even cared for him.

"You two boys chat. I have to tend to some lady business if you know what I mean," she said, heading away from them.

"Liz!" Will shouted. "You sure you're okay by yourself."

She turned around, nodded, then continued on and said over her shoulder, "I'll be only a few yards away."

Will turned his attention back to Zac. "Sure glad you're okay. I wouldn't have been able to live with myself if something happened to you."

Will helped him to his feet, and they gave each other a hug.

"That's enough of that shit," Zac said, pulling away. "We can't get soft out here, you know. Godzilla's out here."

Will turned away for a second. "Zac, it's real. They're real."

Zac nodded and moved in closer to Will, revealing that he understood Will was serious, their situations, serious. "You mean Chee's right?"

Will nodded. "It's a brand new species. Liz and I saw one in full view. They're huge, absolutely immense."

"What are they?" Zac asked, his tone now also quite serious.

"Some type of enormous primate that has been evolving and thriving up here in relative isolation for quite some time. If I had to call them something, it would be an ice gorilla."

Zac shook his head in utter bewilderment. "Ice gorillas. I never would have guessed in a million years that it was true. This is coming from someone who still surfs and believes that the ancient relative of the great white shark, the massive Carcharodon Megalodon, is going to come up from the depths and literally swallow me whole."

"I hear you. I thought it was a hoax, too, until Liz and I saw one."

"What do we do now?" Zac asked.

The fog began to lift, and visibility increased somewhat, as both men surveyed the land, hoping to see evidence, of anything at all. Will turned and looked at Zac. "My gut tells me we need to get the hell out of here, but my head tells me this is a once-in-a-lifetime opportunity to discover something new, my chance to break free of my head in the sand lifestyle that I've been living in for far too long."

"Now that's what I'm talkin' about," Zac said while high fiving Will, "let's document these creatures, and then we can make the determination at home whether or not to go public with the information."

Liz returned to where the two men were standing. "You boys miss me?"

"Ice gorillas Liz. They're called ice gorillas," Zac said with his arms proudly crossed and grinning.

She looked over at Will. "Nobody on this planet knows they're here, do they?"

Will nodded. "A man named Chee does. The thing is, will we make it out alive to enlighten anyone else?"

Chapter Sixty-Two

Peter stood at the bottom of an extensive cave system, completely immersed in darkness. He had never been so afraid in his entire life. Always having been the one in complete control of his life, those around him, and his surroundings, he wanted to curl up into a little ball like a baby and find a place to hide in this darkest of places.

"Are you out there?" he whispered, afraid to raise his voice for fear of luring any potential creatures out of hiding.

He listened for a brief moment, as his hearing had become more acute while his other senses became worthless. Nothing but the sound of water dripping and draining off the sides of the ice cave greeted his eager ears. He listened intently, hoping to hear some sign of Chee.

He took conservative steps, inching his way forward with his arms extended. He moved slowly for quite some time until he lost track of how far he had walked. A question rose in his head that made him come to a complete halt. If he couldn't see a thing, where in the world was he going? The thought of pits, crevasses and hell entered his head.

A noise caught his attention from close by. He stood deathly still, trying his best to make out if the sounds of scurrying from close by were from a human or not. Whatever it was that made the noise, Peter all of a sudden felt the presence of something standing and breathing directly behind him.

Chapter Sixty-Three

The clouds hung low above the massive, one hundred fifty-five square mile ice shelf. The temperatures were dropping by the minute.

Realizing they couldn't afford to spend much longer outside in the elements, Will, Zac, and Liz zinged across the open ice on two snow-mobiles in search of the elusive research center. Their GPS unit indicated the distance to be fifteen miles away.

They had agreed that it wasn't wise to return to their original campsite for fear of encountering the others. Chee couldn't be trusted, and as Will was strangely learning, neither could his once good friend Peter Miles. Jonathon was just a plain liability.

The snowmobiles crisscrossed the ice as Will led the way, while Liz and Zac brought up the rear.

"Shit!" Zac shouted to Liz while hanging on to her, "watch where you're goin'!"

Liz laughed out loud. "Just shut up and hold on!"

"Women drivers!" Zac fired back.

Will looked over his shoulder, as he now had created some distance between his snowmobile and theirs. He eased up on the throttle and began to zig zag slightly in an attempt to let the trailing snowmobile gain ground. As his snowmobile was now traveling at a slower pace, he became more in tune with the environment. Soon he was noticing every crack, crevice, and bump that he ran over. *Lots bumpier than one would think out here.*

Suddenly, Will's snowmobile hit something hard, sending him into a headstand in the air before his backside eventually found its way back on to the seat.

Something's not right, he thought, bringing the snowmobile to a complete stop.

"What's he doing?" Zac yelled.

Liz stepped on it. "I don't know!"

She brought her snowmobile to a stop right next to Will. He didn't say a word to them nor did he even acknowledge their presence. Both Zac and Liz looked at one another in bewilderment.

"Will!" Zac shouted.

He didn't even so much as blink at the sound of his good friend. "Will!"

Will held his hand up while gazing out onto the horizon. "Something's wrong!"

Liz was confused as she looked at him and then out over the ice, which now was shimmering with glare. The until now, absent sun, reflected in all directions against the white backdrop of the land.

"Will, tell us!" she demanded.

As Will turned to address them, the land began to violently shake. "Earthquake!"

None of them could speak, as the ice shook with a force that no one had ever experienced. It felt like the entire world was coming to an end and all hell was breaking loose.

Will saw a crack in the ice that ran due south of where they were standing. It appeared to come to an end several hundred yards away. Cracks of all shapes and sizes were forming and developing all around them. It quickly became apparent that the whole region was in danger of literally crumbling into pieces.

"Stay put!" Will shouted over the deafening roar.

No one knew or quite understood what was happening, just that this was something that was violently shaking the surroundings to the core. A crack began forming between Will and Liz as she screamed. "Will!"

He reached out just in time to snag her back to his side. The rift in the ice quickly opened wide allowing them to see down to the chasms below and what would have been a certain death had they fallen in.

"Zac!" Liz shouted, noticing that he was now separated from the two of them. The opening in the ice had grown to some twelve feet wide and was horizontally lengthening by the second.

The cracks continued to rip through the ice as Zac looked around his surroundings and took a few steps back. He remembered that he had competed in long jump in high school. His hopes were dashed of long jumping to the other side where Liz and Will stood as the rift continued to widen and deepen. He scanned the area while everything now seemed to be happening in slow motion.

Luckily for him, the snowmobile remained stranded with him on his little island of isolation. He jumped on top of the machine. Motioning with his hands, he summoned Will and Liz to hop on their snowmobiles and try to beat the rift, as it continued to grow both lengthwise and widthwise.

The adrenaline coursing through Zac's body made him forget all about his pain. He full-throttled the snowmobile and raced parallel to the rift in the ice, trying desperately to get back to Liz and Will and find a place of safety. Could there still be such a thing?

Will and Liz raced parallel to Zac. They could see the end of the rift, where it had not yet reached. It was a race against both time and Mother Nature.

"Hurry, Will!" Liz said, clinging tightly to his body.

Will gave it everything he had in an attempt to stay neck-and neck-with Zac. Neither driver took his eyes off the path ahead for fear that he might need to veer off at the last second. Zac was intensely focused on the patch of pure and pristine ice some several hundred yards ahead. This would be the place where he could rejoin his friends.

His heart leaped into his throat, as a crevasse suddenly opened a little ways ahead. The snowmobile was moving too fast, and he feared that at this speed any sudden jerks of the machine might possibly cause him to flip over. He couldn't afford to make such a mistake.

Zac's hands instinctively tightened, bracing to jump the open crevasse. His mind could barely process all of this as the ice raced by below him. His body tightened up, as he came upon the crevasse in what seemed like a millisecond.

Chapter Sixty-Four

Peter felt his body go stiff as a board in the middle of what seemed like the heart of eternal darkness. His heart pounded madly, almost to the point that he thought it might burst his chest wide open.

Whatever it was that was behind him could most assuredly sense his heart pounding like a piece of machinery. Most certainly it could smell his fear.

A cold and foreign presence quickly engulfed him, and as he opened his mouth to scream, something muffled his mouth.

"Mr. Miles," the voice whispered, "we are not alone."

Oddly, he found little comfort in the familiar human voice of Chancellor Stephen Chee. He didn't bother to turn around, as he wasn't able to see a damn thing.

Chee whispered into his ear once more. "Our flashlight has gone dead. Mr. Miles, you must see with all your senses. Do not let fear cloud your vision, as now is not the time to be afraid."

Peter took several deep breaths, trying desperately to calm himself. He closed his eyes for a few precious seconds. *Be not afraid, and vision will be granted to you.*

When he opened his eyes, he was stunned to be able to see the vague formations within the ice cave. His head tilted upward, and he could now make out the dens of the ice gorillas that lined the walls of the ice cave. They were endless. The men stood, awed by the sheer volume of dens, indicating that this wasn't one creature, rather possibly hundreds of these giant creatures roaming free above and below the ice.

His eyes had acclimated themselves to the darkness.

"Mr. Miles," Chee whispered, as his head tilted upward toward where the ice vehicle was still wedged in the crevasse some one hundred and fifty feet above them, "we cannot climb out of this predicament."

Peter was shocked to discover that the rope that had allowed them to escape from the ice gorillas above was gone.

"The rope!" Peter gasped, his mind now fully comprehending their predicament for the first time.

Chee nodded. "Once you got down, it suddenly vanished. This is a highly intelligent species, and if we do not act swiftly and quickly, this icy lair will be our tomb."

"There must be another way out," Peter added, "these creatures are incredibly huge, and they must have easy access in and out of this place."

"Exactly, Mr. Miles, but the question is where, and we are running short on time."

Peter's pulse calmed as his senses slowly returned to him. "We'll get out of here. This I can promise you. They may be large, but they're just another species on this planet Earth."

"Mr. Miles," Chee replied, far too loudly, his voice echoing from the far corners of the cave, "do not insult the most intelligent and aggressive creature inhabiting our Earth at this exact moment in time."

Both froze as a terrifying cry suddenly filled the cold icy air.

Chapter Sixty-Five

Zac pulled back on the throttle giving it everything he had with the snowmobile making its way up into the air. Will and Liz looked on while they kept pace on their side of the rift. The snowmobile roared upward and into the icy air. Zac's days as a part time motocross rider paid off. He steadied the vehicle while it made its flight over the crevasse.

The snowmobile slammed down on the other side of the crevasse, Zac's body settling perfectly in place. Seconds before impact, he had relaxed his body so as to minimize damage from the violent impact upon hitting solid ice. He sped forward over the ice, knowing that he had just successfully completed his greatest jump ever. *A perfect ten, bound for X Games glory.*

With a quick glance over his shoulder he saw Liz and Will. To his surprise, the violent shaking of the ice had ceased. He brought his snowmobile to a stop and breathed a momentary sigh of relief. Liz jumped off the back of their snowmobile as they arrived. She gave Zac the biggest bear hug he had ever received in his entire life.

"Damn," he exclaimed, "guess I should jump deadly crevasses every day."

She smiled.

Zac looked over at Will who looked as if he was off in another world.

"What about you, how would you rate that jump?"

Will looked over and shook his head. "Something's not right."

"What do you mean?" Zac replied, "so this place had a little earthquake. Big deal."

Will gingerly got off the snowmobile and walked a few paces. "Look, call me paranoid, but I don't think that was an earthquake."

"How can you tell?" Liz asked.

"I grew up in California, and let me tell you, I experienced my fair share of earthquakes."

Will and Zac looked at each other.

"Then what the hell was it?" Zac questioned.

"I don't know. I have nothing to base my argument on, except sheer gut instinct."

"And there's nothing wrong with that," Liz said, stepping closer to Will, "then what do we need to do?"

Will motioned for them to come in closer, so as not to have to shout over the elements. "Well, for one thing, I think it's safe to assume that we won't see Chee or Peter again. They have gone in search of these creatures, and they will go to the ends of the Earth to find them."

"And Jonathon, too?" Liz added.

Will shook his head and replied, "I've found bits and pieces of Jonathon."

"Bits and pieces?" Liz repeated.

"Yeah, the ice gorillas got him. There is, most likely, nothing left of him by now. I found tattered remains of his jacket, possible bone fragments, and a few other hints of his demise."

Liz had a very disturbed look on her face. "Why didn't you say anything earlier?"

"I didn't want to worry anyone or create a false alarm. Besides, we've had enough to worry about and didn't need anything else on our plates."

"Oh, my God, Will, someone has died? Of course I would have wanted to know." Liz threw her hands up and stepped several feet away from both of them, as if some separation between her and the others would offer understanding.

"Look," Zac said, "I'm not trying to be heartless here, but everyone on this expedition signed up knowing full well the dangers involved."

As if being hit by a bolt of lightning, Zac suddenly hopped on his snowmobile. "You two follow me. It may have just dawned on me what happened."

Chapter Sixty-Six

Peter felt a deep upwelling of primeval fear rise from the pit of his stomach. His ears processed a horrific roar beyond all human comprehension. Chee was frozen, as if stunned by the awesome power of the creatures he had long believed existed. Now at the bottom of their icy lair, they were trapped.

Quickly and quietly they moved through the darkness, trying not be noticed by anyone and anything that may have been at home in their den. Peter could feel Chee's hand pressing into his back as they moved along. He looked up from time-to-time, half expecting to see one of the ice gorillas jumping down from one of the many dens high above them, but no such thing happened.

As they made their way toward what appeared to be the very far end of the cave, Peter's mind made its way back to when he was a child. He remembered the lectures at the local natural history museum that he attended every so often with his older brother. Oftentimes the lectures revolved around the idea of what it would be like to travel back to the time of the dinosaurs.

Many people routinely believed that if one were able to peek back at the time of the dinosaurs, there would be a predator waiting behind every tree, rock, or bush just waiting to pounce on its unsuspecting victims. This wasn't the case for Peter.

Just as today's case with the animal world and top apex predators, one often has to go out of one's way to find a great white shark or twenty foot long crocodile. They aren't lying in wait for us at every twist and turn.

As the two of them inched their way forward, Peter hoped that the ice gorillas were the same.

Chapter Sixty-Seven

As Will sped off in hot pursuit of Zac, Liz sat behind him hanging on tightly. They could see the cataclysmic destruction of all that was before them. Crevasses had formed everywhere, and huge swaths of land were pulverized and fragmented into pieces. They dodged and weaved their way closely behind Zac.

Take deep breaths, Will thought to himself, trying desperately to remain as together and sharp as he could. One wrong turn had the potential of sending them both down a crack to their icy deaths below.

Zac continued to speed over the ice at a blindingly fast pace, never glancing back for a second. As his snowmobile finally exited the maze of rifts and crevasses and made its way out to the smooth open ice, he double timed it. Will increased speed also once he and Liz successfully navigated the maze of death.

Up ahead he could see that Zac had come to a complete stop and was now holding something up in the air, but he couldn't make out what it was, as they were still too far away.

What's he doing? Is he taking GPS measurements? Will thought, catching up with Zac.

Both he and Liz were shocked to discover that they were at the edge of one side of the giant ice shelf. Had they gone any further they would have landed in the frigid waters below.

"I knew it!" Zac shouted, running off at full speed along the edge.

He held the GPS up into the air and then lowered it down so he could read the coordinates. "Shit!"

"Easy Zac," Will said, panting, as they finally caught up with him, "what's gotten into you? What is it?"

Zac peeked down at the GPS again before finally making eye contact with Will. "What's gotten into me is that the unthinkable has happened."

Will still didn't understand. Everyone stood, pondering silently until Liz finally asked, "Zac, what's going on?"

Zac stepped forward ever so slightly, and peered over the edge down to the waters below. "According to our GPS, our camp site should be right here, in these waters."

Neither Will nor Liz spoke a word.

"The shelf broke off, the goddamn ice shelf broke off, and we're floating away." Zac spoke the cold-hearted truth.

Will now knew that everything he thought about the rumble not being an earthquake was true. He lowered his head. "I knew it, I knew it all along. Something inside was telling me."

"How can we be certain the ice shelf broke off?" Liz asked, her voice wavering.

Zac looked down once more. "I've triple and quadruple checked the coordinates. Plus, like Will said, my gut tells me this is what happened. This ice shelf broke away, just like what has been making the headlines for the last decade or so."

Tears began to stream down Liz's face, as the true meaning of the news was finally becoming clear to her. "What do we do?"

Will kicked at the ice. "Shit. I can't believe this."

"Dude, this is blowin' my mind," Zac said, spitting over the edge down to the water below.

He held the GPS up in the air and tried one last time.

Liz and Will looked on, hoping by some miracle that the GPS coordinates would in fact tell them that they were miles off. Zac nodded to himself as he gazed at the screen. "Same result four times in a row."

Will took a few steps away and rested his hands on his hips. Liz walked over and asked an alarming question. "What about the plane?"

Chapter Sixty-Eight

Peter and Chee had instinctively dropped to their knees and covered their heads with their hands, resembling young school children taught to do so during drills. The ice cave shook, chunks and shards of ice rained down around them. They waited out what they thought had been an earthquake, and when looming death no longer appeared to be a threat, they slowly removed their hands from over their heads. Both of them remained on their knees for several moments.

"Mr. Miles," Chee said, "I think it is okay."

Peter quickly stood up and helped Chee to his feet. The two still faced the daunting task of crossing the floor of the cave, now made more perilous by the razor sharp pieces of fallen ice. The vague light allowed them vision, but the cave was massive and depth perception wasn't good.

Peter continued to lead with Chee following with his hand on the man's shoulder.

"What was that?" Peter whispered.

Chee sighed behind Peter's shoulder. "You are asking me a question for which your guess is as good as mine."

Even in the darkness of the cave, Chee noticed Peter shaking his head ever so slightly after Chee had made his comment. *Arrogant asshole. If I could get these creatures on my own, I would. I will leave you here in a heartbeat once I get what I came for.*

Chee suddenly pressed down on Peter's shoulder, "do not move, we are not alone."

Something had run so close that they had felt the gust of wind caused by the close encounter. They could hear the creature still running away from them. Perhaps it had been testing both of them or sniffing them out. It galloped away into the icy silence of the cave.

Peter reached down for his .22 caliber, and his mouth literally fell open, as his hand touched an empty belt loop. *It must have fallen out on the way down here.*

"Shit!" he cursed, his hands now fumbling for the switchblade which he kept in his lower pocket all the way down his right pant leg.

"Mr. Miles," Chee whispered, "human weapons are of no use down here. We are in their territory. Keep your wits about you."

Peter felt a dash of air rise in front of his face as something raced by again. Sounds of galloping and trampling of the ice shards were all around them. It appeared as if they were enclosed in a tight circle that was getting smaller by the second. Peter felt Chee's hand slowly leave his shoulder as the Chancellor stepped away from him. He looked over and could see Chee inching toward the sounds of the creatures pacing and stomping. They sounded like caged lions in the city zoo.

Peter watched as Chee inched his way into what appeared to be the very center of the circle.

Everything was stirring, as if the very cave itself was alive, having been resurrected out of a deep, ancient sleep. Sounds scurried up and down the cave walls, and Peter could swear as he craned his neck up toward the sky that the very roof of the cave was alive with things moving about. He couldn't see for sure, and his attention instantly diverted back to Chee.

Chee stopped as he stood in what he believed to be the dead center. "We mean you no harm." The very sound of his voice echoed throughout the cave.

Peter's eyes opened slightly wider as the sounds and stirring came to an abrupt halt. *It can't be. Are these creatures understanding Chee?*

Chapter Sixty-Nine

The snowmobiles came to an abrupt halt near the edge of the broken ice shelf. Zac quickly jumped off his snowmobile and walked to the edge. Seeing farther long, and the calving edge of the ice shelf into the frigid waters below Zac's eyes grew big.

"Holy Shit!"

Will and Liz joined Zac in witnessing the alarming discovery. Miniature fires were spread out across the water. Black smoke drifted over the area. The shattered remains of the plane, that was to be the team's means of transportation home, was scattered over hundreds of yards of ice and water.

"The plane!" Liz shouted in shock, "how?"

"When the ice broke it must have been in the correct alignment," Zac replied.

"Meaning wrong alignment." Liz shot back.

Will turned away. "We have to get to that research center."

"But if it's gone?" Liz argued.

"We have to try. We have no other choice but to keep looking."

As Liz followed Will to the parked snowmobiles, Zac viewed the calving ice splash down into the frigid waters. *We're not gettin' off, dead or alive.*

Chapter Seventy

Will and Liz sped along the open terrain, following Zac, who held the GPS. All Will could think about was getting to the research center as it appeared to be their only hope of survival. Suddenly, something made Liz look behind them.

"Will!" she shouted, as two white shapes had now come into view some ways back. Several hundred yards behind their snowmobile, white figures were closing the distant gap.

"We've got company, hold on!" Will floored it, literally passing Zac like it was nothing.

"We've got company!" he shouted, passing Zac.

The ice gorillas had now doubled their numbers, as eight of them thundered across the ice in pursuit of Zac who was now bringing up the rear. They cut the distance in half, in no time, and Zac nearly lost control as he turned to take a second look.

"Shit," he cursed, increasing his speed. Several figures now came into an uncomfortably clear view.

That's odd, he thought to himself. *Are the juveniles trying to drive us toward the massive adults?*

For a brief moment, the scientist part of Zac's brain began analyzing and running through the different species throughout time that had utilized juveniles in their hunting strategies. *Predatory dinosaurs used the same tactics.*

His run down memory lane ended when a young ice gorilla lunged and swiped at him with its already huge hand. The snowmobile swerved violently to the left, nearly causing Zac to flip, but he managed to hang on, but was now on a slightly different course from Will and Liz.

Zac's snowmobile quickly got back on track as an ice gorilla lunged at him from the right. The creature's body slammed into the ice, just barely missing clipping the back of the snowmobile as it slid several feet, while Zac sped ahead.

Five ice gorillas were close on Zac's tail causing him to weave back and forth in a desperate attempt to confuse and lose them. They were now only forty feet from the back of his snowmobile.

Liz turned around as her hands gripped Will tightly, fearful of falling off in this most inhospitable of places. "Will, they're almost on him."

Will shot a glance over his shoulder and could see the pack converging on Zac, like lions on the African savannah preying upon a helpless and floundering wildebeest.

"Will!" Liz shouted.

Will's vision was partially obscured by Liz as she held close to him, but he was able to see that Zac had suddenly disappeared from view.

Chapter Seventy-One

Chee lowered his arms as if he had been presiding over the ice gorillas in some strange way. He began to inch, ever so slightly, back toward where Peter was still standing. He took one step after another backward as the entire cave hung in silence.

Moments earlier he had spotted their goal, the route through which both of them would, hopefully, escape to safety. Then they could bring several of these creatures to their knees. Peter remembered that animals have a sixth sense about them that allows them to sense danger.

Chee is an evil presence, he thought to himself. *They should be able to spot it a mile away.*

When Chee was approximately halfway between where he had been standing and where Peter remained standing, he whispered, "now, Mr. Miles." Chee began racing toward the only visible opening in sight. For a moment Peter stood shocked at what he was seeing. Chee ran across the cave floor as everything in sight, human and otherwise, looked on. Peter watched until finally coming to his senses, and began racing in Chee's direction.

The chorus of noise picked up the minute Peter left his spot, and the area was once again filled with every sound imaginable.

Just keep running, his senses expecting at any time to be tackled and devoured.

His eyes were locked keen ahead, as the Chancellor was making his way into the opening. A loud BOOM from somewhere behind him shook his nerves but he continued to run. *What the hell was that?*

The entire area was a cacophony of sound as every noise echoed off every facet and wall of the cave.

As Peter neared the opening where Chee was waiting, a flash of blurry colors from above caught his attention. Still in full panic mode, he dared not look up, but he could see the blur of colors moving.

"Mr. Miles, dive!" Chee shouted, with Peter some fifteen feet from the opening that stood about six feet tall and couple feet wide. Peter, his days of playing collegiate baseball now on full display, dove head first into the opening with reckless abandon. His body smashed down on to the cold damp ice, slid for several feet and toppled head over heels several times.

The BOOM that followed his arrival into the opening was ear shattering and the ice quivered under the immense weight of something. As Peter rose to his feet, he and Chee stood in awe at what they thought they were looking at. Before them stood two massive legs, each as big as a tree trunk and white as the ice shelf itself.

"Dear God," Peter gasped, realizing that they were staring head on at the massive legs of one of the ice gorillas. They were in the presence of the alpha male of this pack of creatures.

Chapter Seventy-Two

"Do you see him?" Will asked, banking the snowmobile and heading back toward where they thought Zac would be.

Liz tried, but all she saw was a dense circle of juvenile ice gorillas, a sight that did little to settle her worst fears.

"Anything?" Will asked, continuing to make a wide circle around where the juveniles were gathered.

Liz remained focused on the small gathering and it looked like they were peering down at something. Her imagination began to run wild, expecting that at any second the mutilated corpse of Zac would be revealed.

"I think he's…."

Will continued to make his wide circle, focused on the terrain and terrified that they would fall through a crevasse if he dared take his eyes off the terrain.

"Do you see him?" Will's voice giving off great desperation for the fate of his friend. "Liz, do you see him?"

"He's gone! I don't see him. The snowmobile is gone, too."

"Where did he go?" Will demanded, "he disappeared."

Both Zac and his snowmobile were gone.

Chapter Seventy-Three

The alpha male ice gorilla bent down and peeked through the small opening in the cave. When it spotted Peter and Chee, it didn't know whether they were friend or foe. Thousands of years of primal instincts were now churning over and over in its brain.

It was far too large to squeeze its body through the opening, and as it retracted its head, the creature stood up and let out the most aggressive of calls to everything in sight. Chee and Peter looked at each other and instantly began to dart further back into the cave, in the opposite direction of the alpha male.

The call from the alpha male was a rally cry for all juveniles to come forth, to hunt and to track down the two humans. No adult ice gorillas could fit their enormous bodies through the opening where Chee and Peter were spotted, and it would be up to the juveniles to tackle this.

Dozens upon dozens of juveniles began storming the floor of the cave, some jumping down from the dens high above while others were already answering the call to duty by flooding through the cave opening itself. Biting, snapping, and pushing prevailed as all tried to squeeze and fit their way through the small opening. The pursuit of fresh human meat, and, more importantly, the challenge of an intelligent kill.

Sounds were everywhere as the walls of the cave were eerily alive with haunting calls while Chee and Peter made their way further back into the cave system.

The juveniles poured into the opening, so much that several, in fact, got stuck. Eventually, they made their way through as the sides of the opening broke away, and bits and pieces crumbled down onto the ice. It was now a mad dash as the juveniles galloped in pursuit of their two human victims.

Chapter Seventy-Four

Zac's lifeless body lay several feet from his snowmobile with blood once again streaming down his face.

Blood. His eyes instantly saw the crimson blood in tiny droplets on the pristine white ice.

Where am I? He looked around, but was severely disoriented.

His hand made its way up to his face where he was bleeding and hurt. He winced in pain as his face had suffered a blow of some sort.

"Another gash, that's all I need. There goes the cover of GQ," he muttered, attempting to climb to his feet before falling down helplessly.

The sound of scratching and clawing from above drew his gaze upward. The first thing that greeted his eyes were the dark black claws of the ice gorillas above, scratching and clawing, trying desperately to free the snowmobile trapped several feet below the ice. He had fallen through a crevasse.

His snowmobile was trapped between the sides of the walls forming the crevasse, just slightly out of reach of the juveniles. However, they seemed insistent upon removing it, feverishly reaching down unsuccessfully, with their long arms and razor sharp claws.

Zac slid along the ice until he was able to rest his back against the wall, his eyes fully focused on the creatures above him the entire time. He knew he had to take stock of the situation. He checked his arms, legs, and then his feet for injury, the feet that had taken him on one adventure after another in the world. From climbing the face of Half Dome in Yosemite National Park, to class 5 whitewater rafting in crocodile infested rivers in Costa Rica, he seemed to have done it all at quite a young age.

Come on, feet, don't fail me now.

Chapter Seventy-Five

Will and Liz stopped a safe distance from the group of juveniles attempting to pull the wreckage from the crevasse. They could see that the opening in the ice was small and barely larger than Zac and the snowmobile. Therefore, the need for the removal of the snowmobile was imperative before the juvenile ice gorillas could make their way down to where they both believed Zac to be.

"Will," Liz whispered, having frantically caught something moving on the horizon and closing in fast on the juveniles.

A gigantic ice gorilla was galloping on all fours, covering huge patches of ice with mind-blowing speed and efficiency, leaping in huge bounds.

Will studied it for a moment, his heart rate increased tremendously as the creature pounded across the terrain. He didn't know whether the ice gorilla was heading straight for them or for the gathering of juvenile ice gorillas.

"Will!" Liz shouted, gripping his shoulders, "over there."

They could see another ice gorilla coming in from the other direction at an equally fast speed. Time seemed to stop for Will, as his mind was processing everything in slow motion. He watched as both creatures galloped on all fours, in the exact way silverback gorillas in the Congo region of Africa had been known to charge at humans.

All four of their limbs worked in perfect accord. These were not creatures of myth or lore. This was a newly-discovered species in the world of science that was now moving at an incredibly fast speed.

"Will!" Liz shook him violently at the shoulder, "they're not headed for the juveniles. They're headed straight for us."

The snowmobile turned over a few times but wouldn't start. Something was shot inside the machine.

They quickly jumped off and made a mad dash for cover. Oddly enough, Will felt no terror in his body at all as they scrambled their way across the ice. What he did feel was a sensation and a feeling for which he couldn't have prepared himself, something that he had never experienced before, or even ever thought he would feel for that matter.

It's hopeless. We're going to die out here. We can't outrun these things, and there's nowhere for us to go. The sense of desperation and hopelessness hit him so hard that for a split second he actually felt as if his knees would buckle under his own weight. His most powerful mind that always kept him calm, rational and scientific all of a sudden failed him. It was gone and proved useless, unable to function efficiently and logically so that they could find a way to save themselves.

By the grace of God, he didn't know why his legs didn't buckle under him, but they kept his body in forward motion as he and Liz were still being chased. Liz looked over her shoulder and could tell that the ice gorillas had easily cut the distance in half. *It's only a matter of time now.*

Will looked over at Liz, and she returned the glance as their tired legs trudged on. Neither said a word, but each knew what the other was thinking. They were going to die horrific deaths as the ice gorillas would most likely rip them limb from limb.

Hopefully, it'll be quick, Will thought, now feeling the burn in his legs.

Tears began to stream down Liz's cheeks. Fate was setting in as quickly as they were being chased. *This was it! The beginning of the end.* Will's mind had already accepted it. Thankfully, he had no children, no wife, no career for that matter. His father had passed away when he was a child. His mother, unfortunately, would be left to deal with the blow of the death of her only son, if anyone found out about it.

Will's body suddenly felt weightless, the burning sensation in his legs had left him, and for some strange reason he felt content. The pain of the mad dash across the ice was now a distant memory, as his brain tried desperately to make sense of the weightless sensation he was currently experiencing.

Chapter Seventy-Six

Peter could barely see Chee ahead of him, as he made his way through the tight and narrow passages of what appeared to be some sort of tunnel, an extension off of the cave. He knew that down here in the confinement of it all, he wouldn't be encountering any of the adult ice gorillas. Yet he almost wished he were dealing with them. The juveniles were unbelievably speedy and agile, and he could hear their cries and shrieks not far behind him. Every sound they made echoed off the tunnel walls as he ran.

Light shown in from time to time, making visibility possible in what otherwise would be an incredibly dark place. He wondered how it was possible, but he didn't let his mind drift that far. After all, they were being chased by the most deadly of predators.

The sounds were getting closer, as if they were just around the corner. He kept telling himself to stay focused, that they were farther back than that.

Man, they sure sound close.

Chee interrupted his thoughts, with his voice bouncing off the walls of the cave, "Mr. Miles, you are almost there."

Peter instinctively sped up and ducked down just in the nick of time, barely missing a sharp edge that was hanging down from the ceiling of the tunnel. He continued onward as the sounds behind him seemed ready to completely swallow and engulf him. A sense of astonishment came over him, as the narrow passageway all of a sudden opened up into a large room. His eyes instantly caught the ray of light that was beaming into the darkness of the room.

A steep slope of tightly packed snow led up and to the opening which led out to the surface. At the very top of the slope was Chee just about ready to squeeze his body through to the outside surface. Peter waved Chee on, signaling him to head through the opening.

Now, in the middle of a very large portion of the underground cave system, he was almost halfway toward the slope that led up and out of the cave when the first of the ice gorillas made its way out of the narrow and confined tight tunnel. *Shit.* He didn't even bother looking as he could hear the animal behind him. His eyes remained intensely focused on the snow.

Peter ran as fast as his legs would carry him across the floor of the narrow tunnel inside the cave. The pain would have been unbearable if it weren't for the adrenaline that was coursing through his body.

The creature that was fast on his tail felt no pain, rarely ever tired, and at the juvenile size of 500 pounds, was already the size of a modern day adult silverback gorilla. It could travel at speeds that no modern day gorilla could ever dream of attaining.

Peter's feet hit the beginning of the snow pack at the bottom of the slope. *Don't slip.* His pace had slowed down just a hair, and his initial thoughts were of course that he would instantly slip.

He could hear the ice gorilla breathing heavily behind him, and his pulse quickened as the sound of more juveniles pouring out of the narrow opening and into the cave could be heard. The cave was now a riot of noise and shrieks as Peter scurried for his life up the snowpack. He struggled with each step that he took.

By now his mind was racing and spinning. He couldn't make sense of anything. The walls of the cave were alive with noise as he closed in on the last twenty feet to the opening. The grade became steeper toward the top, and Peter shouted in a desperate attempt to pump himself up, as he shuffled upwards. "Come on!" His voice was drowned out by that of the ice gorillas.

Shit, they've hit the snow. He turned his head around just for a brief second to see the entire pack now hitting the first part of the snow. His mind instantly raced back in time. *Where did the first juvenile go?*

Chapter Seventy-Seven

Zac neared unconsciousness, fighting to keep his eyes open. *Don't give up, man, don't give up.*

The words of the late, great, college basketball coach Jim Valvano rang in his head. "Don't give up, don't ever give up."

At a time when he needed his most solid and fundamental thinking, he could feel the life leaving his body, as if all the energy that made up his life to this point was exiting, via his fingertips. His hand slid along the cold ice. He could feel nothing, not even the bitter cold.

Stay awake, must stay awake. His eyes blinked heavily several times while the ice gorillas could be heard up above. Exhausted, freezing cold, starving, dehydrated, and losing his urge for survival by the second, Zac made the executive decision to close his eyes, if only for a moment.

As his eyes closed his other senses took over, as his ears could still hear the creatures above him. The darkness and cold soon overtook him.

Chapter Seventy-Eight

I'm falling. Will's mind suddenly recognized, as he continued to fall. He then slammed into the ice. He saw Liz slam hard into the ice. In agony, he tried to turn over.

"You okay?" he muttered over to her. Still reeling in agony, he continued to try to roll over several times until finally he was on his back. He could then see the opening in the ice through which they had both fallen.

The ice gorillas. His mind vividly shot back to the creatures they saw moments prior to falling through what appeared to be a weak spot in the ice above. His eyes remained fixed on the opening above them, expecting the two ice gorillas that were thundering across the open to appear and rear their ugly heads while peering down at them.

"Will," a familiar voice said from close by.

He turned over to see Liz smiling at him. "Man, it's good to see your smile. Are you hurt?"

She shook her head. "I'm okay. You?"

"Lower back is sore, but then again my lower back is always sore."

Liz's eyes darted toward something in the far corner. "Over there."

Will slowly got himself to his feet and proceeded to help Liz stand. They stood, somewhat dumbfounded, as they saw several openings of different sizes. The first opening to the far left was slightly taller than six feet in height, the middle one measured in at around ten feet, and the third opening was a staggering twenty five in height.

They looked at each other and then gazed up at the hole above them.

"I don't believe we have a choice. We need to pick one of these openings," Liz said.

Will put his hands on his hips, his trademark pose for deep thinking.

"You look like you're trying to split the atom. I say let's just flip for which one and hope we come out on the right end."

He gave her a rather serious look. "I say we take the middle one. My gut is telling me that one, and so far in life I've learned that my instincts are usually right."

Her eyes lit up. "You're right. That's why you're addressed as Doctor, and I'm just Liz."

"You'll be called Doctor one day," his eyes still intensely focused on the three openings.

He pointed toward the left one, as Liz followed with her eyes, gazing into the dark opening, wondering what in the hell could possibly be awaiting them. *What nightmares await in those deep and dark places,* she thought to herself.

Will's hand pointed toward the middle opening and then finally the opening on the far right. He scratched his chin and looked up at the ceiling above them, some thirty feet up. He then looked at all three openings once again.

"The middle one," he said while confidently pointing to it.

Liz stepped forward and squinted intensely, trying to see beyond the veil of impenetrable darkness. "You sure?"

He looked up once more at the ceiling, then closed his eyes and tried to visualize the landscape above them. When he opened them, he turned and smiled at her. "The middle one it is."

Liz cracked a wry smile. "Okay, then. You go first."

Chapter Seventy-Nine

Where's the first one?

Peter's mind was frantic, as the entire group was now gaining their way up the slope toward him. The sounds behind him were terrifying.

The opening to the surface was only ten feet away when suddenly the original juvenile ice gorilla came flying down off the wall above him.

"Oh, shit!" In the blink of an eye he ducked. The juvenile sailed past him and Peter hit the ice rolling. It then flipped over and tumbled down the slope, picking up speed rather quickly, it plowed into the group of juveniles making their way up the slope. Like bowling pins they fell in all directions, with the exception of one lone juvenile who continued to make its way up the left side.

It bounded up the slope after Peter, taking one last look down the hill. The sight of the creature rocketing up the hill caused him to push his body awkwardly through the opening, but a piece of his clothing became stuck on a shard of ice.

"Come on!" he shouted, tugging desperately at it, "come on!"

The ice gorilla was gaining on him, its mouth salivating with the thought of the first bite of him, hard on its mind. A primal need drove it up that slope, a memory of a time when the species of ice gorilla first crossed an ancient land bridge and set foot in this land. The first kill in the new land was, undoubtedly, the biggest and baddest they had ever seen, the polar bear. It was here, many tens of thousands of years ago, that this species of gorilla began to develop the taste for meat. Feeding on abundant food sources of polar bear, wolf, and the occasional seal allowed the species, over time, to grow to massive proportions.

Peter was still perched precariously at the opening, with one leg free and the other stuck, as an enticement for certain death.

The ice gorilla could almost taste his kill now as it closed to within ten yards. The panic of his intended victim was evident. The only thing left was to finish him off.

With everything he had, Peter tugged away at his right pant leg, but it was caught. Seeing the ice gorilla fast approaching, he mustered every bit of strength and screamed as loud as he could at the thing.

"Get out of here!" the decibels of the scream nearly searing his vocal cords.

The ringing of his voice against the cave walls did little to slow the ice gorilla as it charged toward him. Incredibly, a hand reached out to him from the surface and pulled him violently through the opening tearing his skin and clothes against the jagged edges of the opening.

Chee stumbled back as the ice gorilla raced straight up to the opening, trying viciously to push itself through, its mouth partially exposed, saliva dripping off of its razor sharp teeth. The creature was too large for the opening.

Chee looked over at Peter, lying on the ice. "Mr. Miles, I told you to stay close."

Peter looked at the opening, the creature now gone. "Yeah, well, I didn't think you could move that fast. What gives?"

Chee shrugged his shoulders. "There is something you should know that I will not withhold from you."

"Huh?" Peter asked, somewhat confused by the off-the-wall statement.

Chapter Eighty

In pain, Zac opened his eyes. He felt the cold and wet hit his body hard. He slowly blew into his hands and attempted to awkwardly rub them together.

Why not, he thought to himself, shaking his head, knowing his hopeless situation.

"Help!" he shouted at the top of his lungs.

He waited for the echo of his voice to die down before he eagerly listened for a response.

"Help?"

He once again listened for any and every sound in response to his cry.

"This is ridiculous."

Out of nowhere, Zac could hear a faint human voice.

"Zac!" the voice shouted.

As if being hit with a shot of adrenaline, his morale picked up, and he slid his body along the ice in the direction of the voice. His eyes had finally adjusted to the dim lighting.

Zac lay there befuddled, staring at the opening to three narrow tunnels within the cave system. He rubbed his eyes, almost not believing what he was seeing.

How long have those been there? What the hell is this place?

"Zac, can you hear us?" the voice said echoing.

"Will. I'm pretty banged up! Are you guys okay?"

"We're fine. Stay where you are. We are coming for you."

Zac chuckled to himself. *Not like I'm really mobile here and can move about myself.*

He looked around, studying his surroundings. Water dripped and the temperature was chilling him to the core. *Man, I gotta get to the Bahamas, and soon.*

Chapter Eighty-One

The massive ice shelf moved through the frigid waters of the Arctic as a huge, unstoppable force. It continued, heading unknown, isolating the entire expedition and everything on it as the huge landmass refused to be stopped.

It had broken off, from north to south, in a sixty square mile slab. For years the ice shelf had been showing signs of instability both in terms of its structural integrity and its rapidly increasing levels of melting.

Chapter Eighty-Two

Will looked into the dark middle tunnel. It appeared timeless and deathly still. "We have no choice. We need to get Zac to the research station ASAP."

He stepped forward and the darkness instantly engulfed him. Liz stood frightfully still, afraid to move a muscle.

Will's hand came out of the black and touched her arm. She grabbed it in a hurry.

"Don't let go of my hand."

Liz nodded and gripped his hand tightly. "I won't, don't worry."

Will tried to recall all the movies in which characters were forced to use all their senses except sight. Neither of them could see a thing. It was completely dark. As the database in Will's mind began filing through all the movies he had seen that required their heroes to see with all senses except their eyes, all he could come up with was the 1987 blockbuster movie, "Blood Sport," starring Jeanne Claude Van Damme. In the movie's final fight scene, Van Damme's character had a nasty powder substance thrown in his eyes. He was forced to fight for a short time with his eyes closed, using only the sense of hearing to detect where his opponent was.

Will shook his head and chuckled to himself in the darkness. *Lot of good a fight scene will do us here.*

"What's so funny?" Liz asked, still maintaining a death grip on his right hand.

"Nothing. Just thinking to myself."

"Well, whatever it was, think about us getting the hell out of here. Will, I'm scared. How do we know that we won't walk right over a ledge and plummet to our deaths?"

As soon as she had asked that question, she heard the sound of something tapping and scratching on the ice in front of them. "What's that?"

Both stood there in stunned silence, as if waiting for the ancient and evil forces of the tunnel to be awakened by their voices.

Chapter Eighty-Three

"Mr. Miles, a little while ago we experienced a rather large jolt and shake."

"Yeah, I noticed that little shake, damn near knocked us off our feet."

Chee strode past him. "It was more than just a jolt. The entire ice shelf has broken off, and we are currently adrift."

Peter brushed himself off and rose to his feet. "A little adrift?"

"We knew this ice shelf was dangerous," Chee responded back.

Peter's rage had met a boiling point when he came dangerously close to Chee. "You knew this ice shelf to be dangerous, that it could possibly even break off, and you put us all in harm's way?"

"Mr. Miles, keep your temper to yourself. After all, we are not alone," he said, studying the horizon.

"I can't believe this shit!" Peter shouted, kicking the ice.

"Mr. Miles, you are underestimating me. I will make this time worth your while, and for your troubles so far, I will double your share for this venture."

Peter's ears perked up and his temper, all of a sudden, calmed. "Double?"

"Yes, double. And by my calculations that will put your share near a value of $1.5 million, before taxes of course."

"Fucking taxes," Peter mumbled under his breath.

"One more thing, Mr. Miles. Assist me until the end, and help me capture one of these ice gorillas, with no questions asked, as to what I do, or my motives, or methods, and I will make sure your share is paid solely in cash."

Peter nodded with a wry smile.

Chapter Eighty-Four

Zac scanned his dark surroundings. The roof of the cave towered thirty feet above him. Seconds later he saw the three incredible tunnel openings that lay some thirty yards away.

Those aren't a coincidence, he thought to himself. *It's not as if water formed this place over millions of years. These were created. Did the ice gorillas do this?*

The sound that came from the far left tunnel caught his attention. It was the largest of all the tunnels, extending up some thirty feet. He thought at any second the figure of a towering adult ice gorilla would come plunging out of the cave and straight for him. He kept listening.

Where the hell are Liz and Will?

The sounds kept getting closer and closer, but still Zac couldn't make out what it was that appeared to be traveling down the tunnel, until it was too late.

"Oh shit!" he shouted, scooting backwards on the ice, still unable to stand.

The sound of a wolf howling could now be heard, possibly two wolves.

"Shit."

As the sound drew nearer, his eyes darted back toward the middle tunnel, hoping to see Will and Liz emerge at any second.

Come on. Hurry up. Where are you guys?

As the sounds grew nearer, he fumbled around with his hand on the ice trying to grab hold of anything sharp, anything at all.

Chapter Eighty-Five

Will and Liz had been walking at a brisk pace for quite some time, totally immersed in the darkness of the tunnel. Will had been relying solely on his senses, walking, and prodding at the ice in front of him. He was using his acute vision which had gone totally into darkness mode.

The tunnel had been eerily quiet for quite some time, as if the walls themselves were watching their every move, waiting for the opportune moment to strike.

The bark and howl of something up ahead broke the silence, stopping them dead in their tracks.

"What is that?" Liz whispered.

Will held up his hand, "that's strange, it sounds like wolves."

His mind began racing with possibilities. *What were wolves doing down here in these caves? Where exactly are they, and do they pose a threat?* The sound of howling could again be heard, and it was definitely wolves. Yet, where were they, and were they coming toward them or going in the other direction?

All of a sudden Liz began shaking Will's shoulder, "Zac."

In an instant they determined that the noises appeared to be coming from the direction where Zac's voice had come. Will grabbed Liz's hand and continued down the tunnel, this time at a faster rate, toward Zac through the dark.

Chapter Eighty-Six

The fog had now lifted and visibility was spectacular. Peter and Chee quickly made their way from the small opening that had allowed them to hastily make their escape from the creatures below. The whiteness of the ice shelf against the backdrop of pristine blue sky made even Chee stop for a brief second. "Mr. Miles, give me a moment."

Chee took several deep breaths of the air, as if he was trying to soak in every moment, experience, breath, and image all at the same time. Peter rolled his eyes and stared out at the skyline, trying to see if he could get a sense if the ice shelf was, in fact, moving, adrift from the mainland.

He shook his head. It was no use. *Do I trust him?*

Peter looked over at Chee who was still taking deep breaths. *That's it, you idiot, keep taking deep breaths. We're only stuck on this goddamn thing. I'll let you know when the ice gorillas emerge and are breathing down our necks.*

Chee let out a great sigh of contentment and then turned and faced Peter. "Shall we? My contact knows of our current plight and has alerted us we are only two miles from the research center."

"Incredulous," Peter exclaimed, "someone's tracking us?"

"Yes. I have my ways. We must get to the research center before the next storm hits. Time is of the essence."

Chapter Eighty-Seven

Zac's eyelids fluttered as he neared unconsciousness again.

Must stay awake. They're coming for me. They'll find me.

His eyes gently closed, only to pop wide open as the sounds of animals close by came from the left tunnel. His eyes closed again, too tired and too weak to even bring himself to face the fate that he felt in his heart he was about to suffer.

His death would be a terrible one. The first wolf would come bursting through the tunnel, and with no fight in him it would go straight for his throat, ripping it wide open with its fierce jaws. The second one would then come in to finish the kill, or at least what would be left of him.

Chapter Eighty-Eight

As Will approached what he believed to be the end of the tunnel, the darkness turned into dim light. He saw the backside of the first wolf, heading straight for Zac's body. Will let go of Liz's hand and began an all out sprint. Lunging at the wolf with reckless abandon, he tackled it and both predator and prey rolled and tumbled end over end.

The wolf tore savagely at Will's clothes, ripping his sleeve clean off. Sensing it had the upper hand, it went right for the throat. Will clamped its snapping jaws with his hands.

The wolf remained on top of him, but he continued to hold the jaws of the fearsome predator with all his might. Both of his hands were wrapped around the animal's snout as it growled and snarled at him.

"Will!" Liz screamed, her voice ringing at a high and frantic pitch.

Will could see the second wolf charging straight for him.

"Shit!"

The second wolf bit down hard just as Will momentarily closed his eyes, waiting for the pain.

Remarkably, the second wolf bit down instead, on the back leg of the first attacker. The first wolf howled in pain as it retreated, while its attacker pounced on top of it.

Territorial dispute, Will thought to himself, rolling backward, closer to Zac who appeared to be coming around. Will got directly in front of Zac, to shield him from a possible attack. They sat in stunned silence as the wolves rolled around and wrestled on the ice. Teeth and claws lashing at each other, each one trying to kill the other.

The second wolf sank its fangs into the back of the neck of the first wolf, drawing copious amounts of blood. The bite inflicted massive damage to the first wolf as it stumbled and staggered back weakly.

Sensing the kill, the second wolf charged and once again drove its fangs into the throat of the animal. It bit down hard, and this time it didn't let go. It remained locked on the throat of the animal as the legs of the first wolf gave way. The second wolf had taken the life of its comrade.

Will stood now, in panicked terror, as the creature paced rapidly back and forth, blood still streaming from its jaws. Will's terror turned to utter disbelief as he saw the wolf turn and focus its attention on Liz. She had managed to go unnoticed, skirting her way along the outer edges of the cave, making her way toward Will and Zac, until now.

The wolf bounded straight toward her driven by the smell of her fear. It was a slave to its primal appetite for flesh and blood.

"Nooooo!" Will screamed, lunging after and missing the tail of the animal.

Liz froze as the animal raced toward her. She put her hands up in self defense, knowing full well that would prove useless against the hungry jaws of this animal. Will started running toward her, just in time to witness the sight of all sights.

Chapter Eighty-Nine

The research center was no more than one hundred yards away and Chee and Peter made good time, given the challenging elements. The storm hit the ice shelf earlier than expected and immersed the two in white-out conditions again. Peter gazed at the old and dilapidated building, almost buried in snow and ice.

Instead of heading directly into what appeared to be the research center's front entrance, Chee veered off toward a second building attached to the main center. Without hesitation, Chee entered the unsecured building.

"Where's the old goat going now?" Peter muttered to himself as he followed.

Inside the building sat a fleet of snowmobiles. Chee approached one of the snowmobiles on the front of the line. "By now our friends down in the caves have alerted everything there to their presence. We must hurry back and collect what we came for. Time is of the essence."

Peter sighed. "You mean me, track down and kill one of these things."

"But of course, Mr. Miles. What do you think I am paying you for? You must earn your keep if you want to reap the benefits."

Peter hopped on the bright spotless, shiny red snowmobile and Chee sat behind him. In the side compartments lay all the ammunition and firearms he would need to achieve this monumental task. They were fully loaded to say the least. Slowly they pulled out, navigating the maze of other snowmobiles that were all perfectly lined up inside the building.

Once out in the open, Peter throttled it and sent the vehicle screaming across the ice. Chee's mind raced with the possibility of conquest. After all these years of tracking, studying, documenting, and believing that this species actually existed, he could feel that fate was on his side. *Today I will not be denied the glory that I so rightfully deserve. This is my moment of conquest and no one else's. It is my destiny.*

Peter sucked in the cold air. His face was continually hit with chilling gusts of Arctic winds and pelting snow. He could feel his body becoming sluggish and quite tired, the entire expedition having taken its toll on him. Peter continued to gulp in the cold air as it seemed to have a rejuvenating effect on him.

They suddenly became airborne as the snowmobile catapulted fifteen feet above the ice. It soared through the air, Peter not quite knowing what to do, or what in the hell had happened.

The weightlessness they experienced was breathtaking as they sailed through the air, the white terrain of the ice beneath them. As Peter braced for the impact, he focused his energy trying to land the back of the snowmobile first and then bringing the front down, just as he had seen time and time again in Winter X Games.

The back crashed down on the ice and he was able to lay the front down softly. The snowmobile streaked again across the open terrain.

Chee looked over his shoulder. Something was on the horizon. "Mr. Miles, control yourself. We have company."

With a quick glance back Peter saw two massive white figures rise up. They were some distance back and were quickly approaching.

"Shit!" Peter veered a harsh right and then back to the left, nearly throwing Chee off.

"Mr. Miles!"

Peter paid no attention, pushing the snowmobile to its maximum. "Are they gone?"

Chee looked back over his left shoulder and couldn't see them. As he brought his head around, he saw the first one on his right. Moving quickly and gaining on them, an adult ice gorilla was closing in from the right side of the snowmobile.

"Mr. Miles!" Chee shouted, "go left!"

Peter quickly swerved to the left, only to discover that another adult ice gorilla was converging on them from the left side of the vehicle. The snowmobile flew across the open terrain as the two creatures galloped behind it, trying with all their might to gain on the small, little vehicle carrying the two even smaller humans.

Peter reached for a firearm from the snowmobile. He managed to grab a small pistol, not enough to take on the massive creatures. As Peter held the pistol up the snowmobile hit a bump and sent the pistol flying.

For the first time in Peter's life, he felt small and insignificant as the two beasts raced just slightly behind them. They were impossibly huge, about eighteen feet tall when standing, and over four thousand pounds in weight. The ice beneath them trembled and shook as their mighty limbs galloped in close pursuit of the humans.

Peter's hands gripped the handlebars like never before as if he was in the chase to end all chase scenes. Without warning, a massive figure rose up out of nowhere some twenty feet directly in front of them.

Peter quickly swerved and frantically overcorrected, but it was too late. The snowmobile flipped over, and time seemed to stand still as their bodies flew through the air. Peter's body was thrown violently. He instantly lost sight of Chee.

His body hit the ice and he slid for what seemed like an eternity before finally coming to rest. The pain was excruciating and Peter lay limp, lifeless, and surrounded by glowing red eyes.

Chapter Ninety

The wolf leaped toward Liz. All she could do was huddle against the wall of the cave with her hands up in a pitiful act of self defense. She awaited her fate and closed her eyes. *God, this is it.*

She heard a snapping sound, like the breaking of bones, accompanied by the howl of an injured wolf. She opened her eyes to the sight of an enormous white ice gorilla, fending off several wolves that were nipping at its back legs, while more wolves poured out of the tunnel and into the cave. Two wolves leaped up and onto the back of the ice gorilla, digging their sharp claws into its back as one wolf went straight for its throat. It leaped up in an attempt to grab hold of the ice gorilla's throat with its mouth, but the massive creature batted it away with its powerful forearms. The wolf was sent flying, hitting the wall, instantly dead.

The two wolves on top tried to viciously rip in to the ice gorilla's back. The ice gorilla threw its body from side to side, trying to rid itself of the annoying parasites.

Will moved slowly, unnoticed, making his way to Liz, skirting around the dangerous attack that was taking place.

He grabbed her hand. "Now's our chance."

They made their way carefully around the battle, hugging the walls of the cave closely. Will could see Zac awake and aware. Sounds meanwhile roared throughout the entire cave.

"We'll have to carry him out!" Will yelled in Liz's ear.

"How do we get out?" Liz replied back, her eyes on the battle as the wolves seemed to be gaining the upper hand.

More and more wolves poured out of the tunnel and there were now six wolves biting furiously at the ice gorilla. The ice gorilla stood fully erect, reaching eighteen feet up in the air, and shook its body, sending the six wolves flying in all directions. Several of the wolves howled in pain as their bodies were flung in to the walls of the cave.

The ice gorilla, realizing it was outnumbered, turned away from its attackers and entered the tallest of the tunnels. Every wolf in sight ran after it, chasing it into the darkness.

"Zac, you have to get up," Will said frantically, trying to lift his good friend up.

"I'm real weak. You guys go. Leave me."

Will shook his head. "Are you nuts? No way! I'll carry you out of here if I have to."

Zac chuckled to himself and coughed a bit at the thought. "You're not strong enough."

Will bent down, paused for a second, made sure to lift with his knees, and promptly hoisted Zac up and onto his back.

"I don't go to the gym for nothing," Will remarked. "Now we need to get out of here. Anything could come out of those tunnels at any time."

"But which tunnel?" Liz said, looking back and forth across all the openings.

Suddenly noises stirred from the far left tunnel, and it appeared to be coming back toward them.

"Quickly, into the right tunnel," Will said, hurrying across the far right of the cave and into the tunnel.

They ran for several hundred feet, until they were well into the tunnel before pausing for a moment. Will turned around, with Zac still firmly on his shoulders, and gazed back toward the opening that led into the massive part of the cave system from which they had just fled. The light illuminated the darkness. Something flashed before the opening as an ominous dark figure could be heard running in their direction.

"Quickly, go!" Will yelled as they turned and ran.

Grunting and growling some distance behind them, the creature was joined by others and their sounds dominated the darkness.

"Will, hurry," Liz said, running some distance ahead.

Liz's shriek from up ahead caused Will to increase his speed down the tunnel. Suddenly, she slammed into both Will and Zac as she had run back to where they were. "They're coming from up ahead!"

Will couldn't see, but the tunnel was soon alive with sounds from every direction. They were trapped. The darkness almost suffocating, as Liz clung to Will who was still holding Zac on his shoulders. Will swung around, and then turned in the opposite direction. Everything was converging upon them at once. Even the walls and roof of the cave were filled with the sound of things racing and scratching toward them.

The three humans huddled close together, out of options and time, they were soon to meet the local inhabitants in a very explosive and intimate manner.

Chapter Ninety-One

Peter woke with a pounding headache. The bleeding gash on the back of his head was huge and painful.

His predicament soon became all too real to him again and it was also apparent that he was being watched. Slowly, he turned his head.

Six enormous ice gorillas had formed a circle around him. They stood some fifty yards from him. His reaction was to stand and make a dash for it, but they had him surrounded on all sides. He knew any sudden movements would surely spell his doom.

The creatures were impressive, each standing over eighteen feet tall on two hind legs, and still an impressive seven feet high at the shoulder while resting on all four legs.

Each ice gorilla was presently resting on all four limbs, looking like gigantic white versions of modern-day silverback gorillas. Each of them had two giant fangs that protruded downward from the back of their jaws, giving them an even more ferocious look. Every single one of them had their powerful forearms firmly planted on the ice.

Peter's breaths were short and shallow. He was afraid to move a muscle, afraid to make a sound.

The ice gorillas sat there, like pristine white statues, not budging, not moving, unperturbed, and yet mighty.

Chee, Peter thought to himself. *Where is he?*

The sound of something shuffling nearby caught Peter's attention. All six of them instantly sprang to life and moved away.

It was Chee. He was trying to make a desperate escape, running awkwardly. The creatures galloped after him, and in no time were quickly on top of him.

Peter, sensing his chance, rose to his feet and raced over to where the snowmobile had thrown them off. With all his strength he managed to get it back upright and in starting position.

"Come on, baby don't let me down."

The engine wouldn't turn over, his hands fumbling desperately to get the machine to start. He continued to try until finally slamming his fist into the snowmobile and kicking at it as he got off. It was no use as the fall had caused engine damage, and the machine was no good at all now.

He could see the pack of ice gorillas moving about over the land, like great beasts reigning over their domain, but there was no sign of Chee. Like a flock of geese, they suddenly turned, in synchrony, and changed their course of direction, their mass now heading back toward Peter.

"Oh shit!"

Peter's first instinct was to make a mad dash for the remaining weapons on the snowmobile, but there was no time. He turned and ran for his life as the pack again set their sights on him. *Where the hell's Chee?* That didn't matter now as Peter fled for freedom and his very existence.

His legs pumped hard, and he could hear and feel the rumble of some twelve tons of weight as the pack thundered after him.

His legs kept pumping, but his brain had almost all but given up. Out in the open terrain, it would only be a matter of moments before they swept him off the ice and devoured him. He was a sitting duck, and with nowhere to run or hide he knew this really would be the end of his life.

Chapter Ninety-Two

The darkness was so absolute in the tunnel it felt as if it were suffocating them as they continued to grip each other fiercely. Zac was now standing, and the three moved together as one toward the left side of the tunnel wall. They stopped as Will's shoulder brushed up against the wall.

The sounds coming from both ends were enough to turn anyone's blood to water. The chilling, scurrying sounds from the roof of the tunnel were particularly alarming.

This is it, Will thought to himself. *After all this, it will be over. We're going to be shredded to pieces.*

Will turned, panicked, as something grabbed at him from the wall. In one big swoop, the three of them were pulled through the wall of the cave. The grinding sound of a great stone slab could be heard closing behind them. Will stumbled over Liz and Zac who had already fallen to the floor.

The deafening cry of shrieks, roars, and chest beatings could be heard from the other side of the stone wall. The creatures were tearing each other to pieces as the three of them scrambled to their feet. Will swiped at the air with his fists as something stirred in the darkness. "Who's there? Show yourself."

Will felt Liz's trembling hand grab his.

"Where are we?" Zac whispered, "and what the hell was it that grabbed us?"

The air was deathly still inside as the battle continued on, just outside. Sounds of utter terror outside made Will's stomach turn, knowing that they were literally seconds away from being torn to pieces, but he took a large breath, sensing an evil presence in the room.

The cold air gave off musty odor. A bright light suddenly illuminated the entire area. They instantly had to shield their eyes which had grown accustomed only to darkness. Will squinted, trying hard to make out the figure before them. It was all blurry, but slowly he was able to discern more details.

It can't be, Will thought to himself, rubbing his eyes, finally adjusting to the light.

"You were expecting an ice gorilla?" the voice asked.

"Who are you?" Zac demanded.

"That's quite an acknowledgement considering that I just saved all of you from meeting your maker out there," the voice said.

The three could still hear the battle outside in the tunnel. It was hard not to notice the fierce battle.

"If you all are wondering what's going on out there," the voice said, "they are battling to the death. They are ripping each other from limb to limb. Survival is for not only the fittest, but the most tactical and cunning. This is the way it has ended for every expedition."

Into the light stepped a man, in his early fifties, with a salt and pepper beard and short grey hair. "Name's Jenkins, Dr. Eb Jenkins."

Will took a deep breath, trying to take it all in, but it was no use. His head was spinning with facts, fear, questions, and the looming urge to get far, far away.

"Dr. Jenkins," Will stuttered, still half not believing what he was seeing. "Thank you for saving us." Will motioned with his hand toward the door that led to the tunnel. "What on God's earth are you doing here?"

Dr. Jenkins let out a great laugh. "Guess the real world just wasn't for me. To answer your question more specifically, it was the chance to study a brand new species, something of which the scientific community and the world at large are not even aware."

"The chance to pad your wallet as well," Zac muttered.

Dr. Jenkins nodded. "I can't lie. That was a major factor as well. The chance to never have to worry about money again is an intoxicating endeavor indeed."

"But who's paying you? Who's funding all this?" Will asked.

It was now evident that they were in a lab, complete with lab coats, computers, books, a desk, refrigerator, and a slew of other equipment.

"The only man who has spouted off about this species for decades now. I must admit I was a bit skeptical at first as well. Just when you think you know planet Earth, something like this literally comes out of nowhere and bites you in the ass."

Will looked on anxiously, waiting for the words that he knew would roll off the tip of Dr. Jenkins' tongue.

"Chancellor Stephen Chee," Dr. Jenkins said.

Will's eyes widened. "I knew it. How long have you been here?"

Dr. Jenkins strode over to his calendar. "Almost two years now."

"Shit, that's a long time," Zac remarked aloud.

Dr. Jenkins nodded. "Indeed it is."

Jenkins pulled back a curtain directly behind his set of computers to reveal a fleet of offroad vehicles, including, among all things, a full-sized Ice Hummer. The room that they were in was much more massive than it first appeared. "I started up here two years ago, under the watchful eye of Chee. He funded all of this. At first, it was supposed to be a study of this new species, but I soon learned that he was fully intent on capturing one of these creatures for his own personal gain."

Zac was busy peering beyond Dr. Jenkins and at the massive space that housed the off road vehicles. "It's like the Batman's cave in here or something."

Dr. Jenkins laughed and nodded at the view behind him. "Indeed it is, but I'm no Batman."

"No," Zac remarked. "But you and Chee are intent on aggressive expansion."

Dr. Jenkins' mood turned sternly serious. "Please sit down, all of you. Can I offer anyone anything?"

No one replied, but he could tell that they were famished. They gorged themselves on energy bars, fruit, water, and some leftover sandwiches he had stocked in his refrigerator. As they ate, he briefed them on the situation.

"Now, I need all of you to trust me and what I'm saying."

Both Will and Liz nodded, their mouths full of food.

"My friends, we are in grave danger. You are, by my account, the fourth expedition to this area, and everyone before you has perished. But not this time. I won't sit back and watch Chee allow you all to put yourselves in a situation from which it is impossible to get out."

Will scooted forward in his chair. "How do we get off this ice shelf?"

Liz looked over at him.

Dr. Jenkins' face had grown steely. "The research center is our best bet for survival."

Will leaned back. "How do we get out?"

"Easy," Jenkins replied. "We commandeer two of the snowmobiles and ride the hell out of this place, never to return to these dismal depths."

Zac's eyes were on the ice vehicles the entire time, and he was chomping at the bit to get out and into one of them. Will had noticed the several television screens that were stacked on top of one another. "Security cameras?"

"They were," Dr. Jenkins replied. "When the shelf broke off, this place was shaken to the core. Felt like the damn end of the world down here. Even lost my bird. It flew away only minutes before it broke."

Liz made eye contact with Dr. Jenkins. "Animals have that sixth sense about them. They know before disaster strikes."

Zac laughed. "Maybe we can just follow the route that the bird took out of here."

Dr. Jenkins' attention was suddenly diverted to the tunnel. All was silent out there. Everything had died down. "Now's our chance. We must move."

Chapter Ninety-Three

Peter had run as far as his legs would take him. Huffing, puffing, and out of breath he hunched over, the feeling of nausea coming on quite strongly now. He looked up, and to his astonishment he was the tallest thing in sight.

Where the hell are they?

He scanned the area once more. Nothing. No sign of the pack of six ice gorillas at all, or Chee for that matter. But then about fifty yards out from where he was standing, something caught his eye.

"Mr. Miles, hurry quickly!" Chee hollered to Peter to move along.

Peter wasted no time, sprinting toward what appeared to be a trap-door, in the middle of nowhere. Chee had the door propped open ever so slightly. "Get in."

Peter climbed down into what looked like a small bomb shelter. "What the hell is this place?"

"Do not ask questions," Chee said, while closing the door on top of them.

The space where they were standing was barely large enough for two men to stand, and Peter at 6 feet 3 inches had to duck slightly. He noticed a ladder that led down, in to the darkness.

Chee had already begun climbing down the ladder, leaving Peter no time to ask questions. When Chee had descended a bit, Peter finally launched himself down the ladder. Figuring he would give Chee a head start, he was surprised to find the old man surprisingly nimble. He was out of sight.

The ladder descended for what seemed like an eternity, and Peter soon lost track of his progress.

"You are almost there, Mr. Miles. Keep going."

The sound of Chee and the thought of all that money gave him the added boost he needed. He flew down the rungs one by one, his feet at long last touching down on terra firma. Peter instantly walked toward Chee. "You have some explaining to do. What the hell is this place? You abandoned me out there to die."

"Mr. Miles, please keep your voice down. We are not alone down here. Answer this. If I abandoned you out there, why are you here now?"

Peter frowned, not quite sure how to respond, but still with the gut feeling that he was right.

Chee crept forward. "It is said, in life that before you help others, you must first help yourself. Up there, I helped myself first before you. And for that, you are now here."

Peter once again had no response. "But you seemed to know where to disappear to up there. Who built this place, all of this?" His hands waved around, still not processing what he was witnessing.

"Mr. Miles, when we upped your deal, you specifically agreed to not question me or my ways. Do we still have a deal?"

He looked Peter directly in the eyes, causing him to hesitate for a brief second. Peter eventually nodded.

"Good," Chee replied. "Realize this. There are many mysteries in the world, some great, some small, some well understood, and some not well understood at all. Am I making myself clear?"

Peter nodded once again. "Yes."

The area in which they found themselves was no bigger than a ten by ten room, somewhere deep within the Arctic ice shelf. It was almost as if it were a holding cell of some sorts.

"We are at the heart of a vast and deep cave system," Chee said, appearing to be deep in thought. "The plans have changed. Originally I wanted one of these creatures. I now want an entire family, complete with the juveniles. Four, possibly five."

Peter sighed a deep breath, knowing full well what it would take to capture one ice gorilla, let alone four or five.

"We are down here because the others will serve as bait. They will bring the creatures to the exact spot where I want them. The exact spot where they are most vulnerable. Mr. Miles, are you capable of this?"

Peter looked up at the ceiling and exhaled.

"Done," he said looking Chee squarely in the eyes.

Chapter Ninety-Four

The team had managed to slide two snowmobiles out and into the tunnel where they had narrowly escaped death. Dr. Jenkins followed and via remote, sent the massive granite door sliding shut. The sound that it made emphasized the fact that they were exposed once again. All appeared to be clear in the tunnel on both sides as they quietly arranged one snowmobile in front of the other.

Jenkins moved to the front. "We must be quick, and we must be quiet. We will have one chance to do this successfully."

The tunnel was approximately one mile in length. They sat directly in the middle of it, with a half mile to the exit. Lighting was poor, but some light still managed to enter in from each end of the tunnel.

Zac had already climbed on the back of Jenkins' snowmobile, half pissed off that he wasn't able to drive this harrowing trail out of the tunnel on one of the Ice Hummers. However, he just sat there in silence.

"Now remember," Dr. Jenkins said, approaching Will and Liz, "you follow as closely as you can. Once we get out of the tunnel, we will veer sharp left. Then we will skirt several more tunnels and take what I call the ramp up and out to the surface."

Will nodded, trying to calm his nerves.

"Oh, and one more thing," Dr. Jenkins said, turning around, "be on guard at all times. Now that the cameras are down, we have no way of knowing where the ice gorillas are. They could be anywhere. Even the ceilings and walls."

"Great," Will sarcastically muttered, "we're already familiar with that."

Liz held him tightly from behind. "We'll be fine. You're going to drive me to safety. Then once on the surface, we'll get back to the research center just in time to be rescued."

If this were a Hollywood ending, Will thought to himself as the snowmobile ahead fired up. As he was about to do the same, a low rumbling could be heard from somewhere behind them.

Dr. Jenkins' head shot around as fast as the sound could be processed. "Now!" he shouted.

He and Zac shot off into the darkness, their headlights illuminating the way.

"Will," Liz said, shaking him.

"It's not turning over."

It was apparent that they weren't alone in the tunnel, as the sounds sent shivers through both of them.

"It's not turning over!" Will shouted, unable to get the vehicle to start.

"Will, they're coming!" Liz screamed, looking back and seeing dark figures of all sorts racing toward them. Her neck snapped back when the snowmobile shot forward when Will finally managed to get it to start. She gripped him tightly as they followed Jenkins and Zac, now a few hundred yards ahead.

The snowmobile raced across the ice as Will veered dangerously close to the walls of the tunnel several times. Liz brought herself to look back once more, fully expecting an ice gorilla to rip off her face. "They're gaining on us, Will!"

The first snowmobile made it out of the tunnel, and Will pushed his machine even harder to try and make up the distance. The walls and roof of the tunnel seemed to pulse as well as they headed toward the end.

Will was intensely focused on the opening, scared to death that the ice gorillas would converge upon them from that direction, thereby trapping them, in what would end in a bloody disaster.

Flashes of shapes began raining down everywhere. The ice gorillas were dropping from the walls and ceiling of the cave one after the other. Will swerved, just avoiding a massive adult, plunging to the ice next to them. The area was swarming with ice gorillas, as the mass had finally made its way out of the tunnel.

Will gunned it, streaking across the floor of the huge cave as the ceiling continued to come to life. One ice gorilla after another began dropping, shaking the place to its very core. Will knew it was only a matter of seconds before they'd be overwhelmed by the masses.

"Will!" Liz screamed, terrified, knowing full well that the ice gorilla was their roadblock between making it to safety and death.

"Duck!" Will shouted, as the snowmobile zoomed right between the legs of the great beast. Up ahead they could see Zac who was now off the snowmobile and peering back toward them and the cave.

Will waved him off. "What's he doing?"

Liz also saw him. She tried waving him off as well, urging him to get out of the area and back on the snowmobile. To their surprise the ice gorillas had not followed them up these last few yards.

As they neared, they could now fully see Zac running toward them.

"Go back!" Will shouted, speeding toward him, "go back!"

Out of the corner of Liz's eye, she saw what Zac had seen all along. An adult ice gorilla was making its way along the walls of the cave toward them, gripping the side walls with almost superhuman strength. Liz shook Will, but it was too late as the creature catapulted itself off the wall toward them. With no time to react, they could only duck and pray.

Zac lunged forward toward the beast. In a blur, Will and Liz saw a confusing array of shapes and sounds as Zac flew in front of them and was snatched by the ice gorilla.

A sharp crunching sound followed as Will and Liz looked on in horror. The ice gorilla and Zac suddenly fell through the ice to the dark depths below. They were both gone in an instant.

Will was numb, driving out on the ice, searching for Dr. Jenkins, but he was nowhere to be seen.

Will managed to find the tracks of Dr. Jenkins that led to where he and Liz believed they would find the research center.

They followed the tracks for quite some time, hardly giving a damn if anything was still in pursuit of them.

Liz could feel Will's pain as they drove on through what was now blizzard like conditions. She continued to hold his body with her arms, wishing to transfer all her love and strength to his body. After witnessing the horrific disappearance of Zac, she knew he was reeling in pain and was holding it all in.

From time to time she would check behind them as they moved on, making sure the coast was clear and trying to be the eyes and ears for both of them.

Finally the research center came into view.

"There it is," he muttered in a trancelike state.

"We made it," Liz said hugging him from behind, trying her hardest to express her enthusiasm that Will had led them to safety and she couldn't be more proud of him. It was of little use though as Will had no response at all.

As they reached the doors of the research center, Will brought the snowmobile to an abrupt stop, prompting Liz to climb off the back.

Will sat there for a few seconds, completely silent and lost in thought.

Liz stepped back quietly, trying to be as respectful as possible. Will slid slowly off the snowmobile, standing up staring at the research center. Liz could feel the tears streaming from her face just looking at him.

Will fell to his knees, as the emotions of the last few years of his life and the terrors of the last days, overcame him.

Chapter Ninety-Five

Peter looked at Chee and shook his head ever so slightly. He was growing increasingly frustrated with the Chancellor, yet he kept his mouth shut. After all, with the success of this expedition, he'd never have to work again. He'd be free to travel, golf, relax, and devote himself to writing fulltime, his true passion and interest in life.

The floor beneath them vibrated as the elevator began its ascent, on the way to a comfortable climate inside the research center. Peter didn't say a word when Chee had them earlier board a horizontal escalator that ran several miles, nearly the entire length of the cave system, very much like the moving walkways in airports.

He didn't say a word when they arrived at another elevator which would take them up to the research center. He was becoming fed up and tired of all this nonsense. However, he continued to hold his tongue and not ask questions. He also wondered how the elevators and escalator were even working given the damage to the ice shelf. *This place must work off of one massive generator of some sort,* he thought to himself.

This will all be over soon, he kept telling himself. *My money will be in the bank and I'll be in the Caribbean somewhere working on my next book. Chee can go fuck himself.*

The elevator bumped several more times and Peter looked over at Chee who was staring at the panel of numbers with anticipation, waiting for the signal that they had made it up to ground level.

Psycho, Peter thought to himself.

The elevator promptly made a ding.

"We are here," Chee said with a smile.

As the doors were opening, Peter couldn't help but wonder what awaited them inside. Chee had briefed him on the situation. Dr. Jenkins should be arriving in one hour with the rest of the team and everything else should follow. It was that simple. The research center was heavily loaded with firearms and ammunition. Peter had been ordered to kill a family of ice gorillas, meaning two adults and two juveniles. The rescue plane was a scheduled military cargo plane, capable of rescuing both Chee, Peter, and four ice gorillas.

The door of the elevator opened. Peter looked up just in time to see a set of red glaring eyes come bursting forth through the doors right at him. Chee managed to slip around the juvenile ice gorilla, lunging with its mouth wide open toward the body of Peter, claws fully extended.

Peter's hands met the ice gorilla's jaw, trying to grab hold of it. The beast snapped at him several times, showing its back fangs. The animal's claws dug into his shoulders, gouging and scraping off huge hunks of his flesh.

Peter screamed, as panic overcame him. The juvenile overpowered Peter and wrestled him to the ground. Peter maintained his hold on the jaws, knowing full well that it was only a matter of time before he couldn't hold it off anymore. The juvenile would then have free reign to devour him in any way that it so desired.

"Shoot it!" he shouted over to Chee, "shoot the fucking thing!"

Chee strode a comfortable distance away from the elevator as the juvenile scratched and clawed at Peter's body, gouging him all over, inflicting serious wounds with each swipe of its claws.

"Help me!" Peter begged as he bled profusely.

The weight of the beast bearing down on Peter was incredible, weighing nearly five hundred pounds, more than an adult silverback gorilla despite being only a juvenile.

"Mr. Miles, do you value your life?"

Peter could hardly respond as the animal was literally, inhumanly strong and he felt his own strength leaving him.

"Yes!" he replied, hardly able to breathe as the animal continued to wear him down.

"I'm sorry, Mr. Miles. I could barely hear you."

Peter pushed with his legs, trying with all his might to budge the five hundred pound creature, but it was no use. He could feel his hands about to lose grip of the jaw.

"Yes," he muttered, "you sick fuck. Now shoot it!"

"Mr. Miles," Chee said, pacing away with his back toward them. "Your services are no longer needed with this expedition. Best of luck to you."

And with that Chee pressed a remote button, closing the elevator door.

The juvenile instantly broke its jaws free from Peter's hands, and went straight for the kill. Peter Miles couldn't even muster a scream for help as the creature wasted no time in ripping his tongue out, swallowing the slippery object down whole. The creature's glowing red eyes met Peter's, as the elevator quietly descended to the depths below.

Chapter Ninety-Six

"We shouldn't have come here," Will sobbed, tears streaming from his face like a child. "And now Zac's gone. How the hell can I go on living?"

"Because he would have wanted you to go on," Liz said, kneeling down and putting her arms around him, "he wouldn't want either of us to die here."

The two embraced for some time before Liz finally helped him to his feet. Wiping the tears from his face, he and Liz fought through the snow and approached the entrance to the research center. Liz slowly opened the creaking door.

"How nice to see you," Chee said, standing there with his arms crossed, "please, won't you come in?"

The room suddenly went black and oxygen became limited for Will and Liz as a giant bag was forced down over both of them. Frantic and desperate to escape the trap, they began striding in all directions, quickly getting turned around in the massive bag. In no time they had managed to get all twisted up, completely enshrouded, and then the struggle ended.

Chapter Ninety-Seven

Will blinked several times before taking in a huge breath of air. He recoiled, his mind sending him back to the memory of being suffocated.

I'm fine. He could see Liz bound to a pole with her hands and feet tied, her mouth taped. He was bound to a pole of his own, with his feet and hands bound, but surprisingly his mouth was free. He could now see Chee staring directly at him. "I can see you are awake. That is good. It would be a pity to lose you now."

Will lunged for him but was held by his bonds. He wanted nothing more than to pound Chee's skull into the ground.

"Mr. Freeman, Mr. Freeman, is that any way to greet me?"

"This whole trip was a lie. You've lied to us all along."

Chee didn't respond, instead began to pace with his hands calmly behind his back.

"Where's Peter?" Will blurted out.

Chee laughed quietly to himself. Will's fury was boiling. "Where is he? What have you done with him?"

Chee's eyes became serious. "Such passion. Such conviction. Such faith and interest in a person who has shown you none."

Will was perplexed and didn't understand the comment.

"Mr. Miles is currently indisposed," Chee said with a chuckle. "Scratch that. He is permanently indisposed and will not be returning to this expedition."

Will had never been very trusting of Chee in the first place, but for the first time, he was now feeling a very sinister vibe from him. It was a deep repressed feeling that he always knew was present, but he had for some strange reason, decided to give Chee the benefit of the doubt. Until now.

"Mr. Freeman, they never caught your wife's murderer did they?"

Will could feel a sickening feeling rising in his stomach. He didn't respond to the question.

"I did not think they did," replied Chee. "Did it ever strike you as odd that Peter Miles, your best friend growing up, did not attend your wife's funeral?"

Will looked over at Liz who was finally awake but couldn't utter a word.

"Pay attention to me, Mr. Freeman," Chee snapped. "Your wife was a good university employee, always watching the school's finances, saving it tens, sometimes hundreds, of thousands of dollars annually. But she became too nosy and threatened to shut down everything for which I had worked so hard. When she questioned me about a large sum of money that was unaccounted for, I knew I had no choice. Something had to be done."

Chee moved in closer on Will. "Evolution is what I like to call it."

Chee took a deep breath, as if he was taking in the moment, almost enjoying making Will sick to his stomach.

"Mr. Freeman, I had no choice. She threatened to put an end to all of this," he said as he waved his arms.

Will's brain was working slowly, but the horror and gravity of the moment hit him like a ton of bricks. "You vile monster."

He lowered his head, absolutely repulsed by the site of Chee, cursing the fact that he trusted him and put not only his life in danger, but his close friends as well.

"Mr. Freeman. On the night of your wife's brutal murder, the man behind the mask was none other than that of the once great, Peter Miles."

Chapter Ninety-Eight

The icy cold sensation that suddenly came over Will's body was one that he had never experienced before, nor did he ever know he could experience something so chilling. His body and mind had gone numb, absolutely and utterly.

Peter murdered my wife, he kept thinking to himself. The thought kept turning over and over in his mind. He wanted nothing more than to confront Peter, but without any sign of Peter, Will's chance of revenge was gone. All Will could think of was the likelihood of Peter suffering his own death delivered by Chee. He would never have a chance at revenge against Peter on his own.

He tilted his head back against the pole, his hands and feet still bound. To his dismay, he glanced over and saw that Liz was gone. A hard object blindsided him as something smashed into his face, sending his head shooting backwards violently against the pole.

Chapter Ninety-Nine

I'm freezing, Will's mind registered, *where am I?*

He couldn't move his arms or legs, and was strapped to an object, something directly behind him. Out in the open approximately a half mile away from the research center itself, Will sat upright, strapped to Liz who was bound and also gagged.

"Liz, is it you?"

She mumbled something indecipherable back, but from those sounds he knew it was her.

"Relax," Will said, "I'll think of something."

The vicious storm had decreased but the bitter cold remained and sent the message to his brain, the message that now was the time for swift action. In an instant Will had figured it out entirely. *They've left us here to die. We're being used as bait to attract the ice gorillas. Chee and Dr. Jenkins will perform the grizzly task of capturing these creatures.*

Will's eyes scanned the horizon, looking for anything and every-thing that could help them. It was devoid of movement, a wasteland of nothingness, yet he knew it was brimming with life. He thought to himself for a moment. *Are Chee and Jenkins sitting in the comfort of the research center, watching us, waiting for the time when the ice gorillas will come?*

The idea came to him, gazing back to the research center.

"Liz, I know you can hear me. I need you to listen carefully. If you are understanding what I'm saying, hit your back to mine three times."

Liz did just that, tapping his back three times with hers.

"Good," he replied, "that's real good."

He took a few deep breaths and gathered himself. "Now, we're out of options, and I know damn well that Chee and Jenkins are watching us from the lab. What we need to do is simple, but we must be convincing by our actions. The ice gorillas like their prey live. They see it as the ultimate test. It's my hypothesis that they won't waste their time with dead prey. Tap your back to mine again if you're still with me."

She did.

"Okay then. I'm going to hold up my hand in the shape of a gun. I'm not going to do it yet, but when we are ready. I'm going to promptly point it at your head. When I give you the word, I need you to make your body go limp, as if you have been fatally shot in the head. Once it appears as though you're dead, I'll do the same to myself. Now I know what you're thinking. If they're leaving us for dead, why would they care if we're dead then? I thought the same thing. This species seems to like things alive instead of dead. I've seen plenty of dead polar bear carcasses that have gone untouched. They enjoy the chance to kill something."

Will paused, trying his hardest to make out any human forms back at the research base. It was no use. If Chee and Dr. Jenkins were there, they were indeed watching from the warmth of the inside.

"When you're ready, touch my back again with yours."

Liz took a few seconds but eventually rubbed her back against his. Will struggled to get his right arm free and in a deliberate motion, he extended his hand in the form of a handgun to Liz's head.

Chee looked on from the research lab. "What is he doing?"

I think it's pretty obvious, Dr. Jenkins thought to himself.

Chee turned and faced Dr. Jenkins with a rather serious look of concern on his face. "You did not check Mr. Freeman for possible concealed weapons, did you?"

Dr. Jenkins seemed stunned by the question. His job had been to deliver the captives to Chee, and he had done just that.

"Your silence tells me you did no such thing?" Chee barked.

Both of them turned just in time to see Will's hand placed directly at Liz's head as the motion of shooting her occurred. Liz slumped over.

"Great Scott!" Dr. Jenkins replied. "I failed to give it a thought."

Chee continued to look on. "Exactly, Mr. Jenkins, you did not give any thought to it. Our success here depends upon every last detail being thought out."

Will raised his hand to his own head and motioned to shoot, promptly slumping over Liz. The two of them just lay there, completely lifeless, and completely devoid of life.

Chee turned away in disgust, having seen enough.

Dr. Jenkins shook his head, knowing full well that his boss wasn't pleased.

Chee turned around for a moment. "Get out there right now. Go clean that up. It is your mess."

Dr. Jenkins shook his head and meandered toward the entrance door of the research center. *What a piece of work he is. One of those shitty abstracts that make absolutely no sense whatsoever,* Jenkins thought to himself.

Chapter One Hundred

Chee made his way straight for the bathroom. He lowered his head and let the cool water splash on his face. It had a reviving feel to it, and he loved every moment of it. For several seconds the water continued to run as he let it cool his face. He reached for a towel on the nearby rack. His mind still raced with the possibility of conquest.

Though his body didn't show it, and his driver's license read 55 years of age, Chee was 67 years old.

I have been at this for a long time, he thought to himself. *Forty years this year.*

Chee's reasoning for concealing his age lay entirely with him, as did most things in his life. He thought back to all the expedition researchers who had perished as a result of his lifelong obsession with the ice gorillas.

"It is not your fault for all those lives lost!" he shouted into the mirror as he pointed at himself. "They accepted the risk of each of the expeditions. The lure of money and greed was too much for their weak and pathetic souls."

He startled even himself with the intensity of his voice, bending down again to rinse his face, hoping to rinse away the pain and burden that all those failed expeditions had brought him over the years. The warm towel across his face felt comforting as he stood up.

Chee meticulously placed the towel on the rack. He returned to the sink and looked into the mirror. In the mirror staring back at Chee was a glowing set of red eyes.

The creature launched itself through the mirror at him as he grabbed his knife from the sink counter. The creature was upon him before he knew it.

Chee drove the knife into the juvenile ice gorilla, as it overwhelmed him. He pushed the weapon in and upward, damaging internal organs. He edged back several feet away from the wounded creature, howling in pain. It staggered toward him on all fours. Chee showed no mercy, driving the knife into the back of the creature's neck.

The juvenile fell to the floor, the sound of five hundred pounds suddenly giving way was impressive indeed. Chee took one look at the juvenile. *This will do just nicely. Now if Jenkins can just get his act together out there, we will indeed be a success. Glory shall be mine.*

Chapter One Hundred-One

As Dr. Jenkins sped across the ice he could see the bodies of Liz and Will just lying there, slumped over one another. He looked at his wristwatch. The rescue plane would be touching down in approximately forty-five minutes. He knew damn well that Chee expected to be traveling back to the United States with at least four extra visitors. Whether or not the ice gorillas were indeed alive at the time of their capture depended on how well the hunt went.

Jenkins slowed the snowmobile down as he closed to within one hundred yards of the bodies. *That's odd,* he thought to himself as he was now about ninety feet from Will and Liz. Jenkins parked the vehicle and decided to walk the rest of the distance. *No blood.*

Standing at an arms' length from the two, he saw no visible signs of death. There was no blood, no trace of anything, just two individuals who were hanging completely motionless as he stood there scratching his head.

Jenkins took a deep breath and looked back toward the research center. *That bastard's watching me for sure, waiting for me to screw up. I know he'll use force to prevent me from entering the rescue plane. He'll leave me stranded here to die. I'll show him. I'll drag the bodies out of here, far away from the ice gorillas. Then he'll be screwed.*

Jenkins made two mistakes as he turned and headed back toward the snowmobile. He planned to tie the bodies together and drag them to a secret location. This would destroy Chee's expedition. However, he had failed to check the bodies to get clarification that they were indeed dead. He also paid no attention to the fact that the supposed handgun was nowhere to be seen. It should have been lying in broad view out on the ice, yet it was nowhere in sight.

The knife struck deep into Jenkins back as Will wielded it with the skill of a marksman. It had been hidden in his sock during the entire expedition. Will and Liz rose to their feet at once, having untied themselves unobserved as Jenkins was boarding his snowmobile back at the research center.

Jenkins had fallen to his knees as the knife protruded from his back. The knife was deep, as he struggled to breathe. Will came around front to view his victim. Jenkins gasped as he was now seeing Will head on, and Liz standing next to him.

"We trusted you," Will spoke. "You left us to die with that psycho. Now it's your turn." And with that he yanked the knife from Jenkin's back and reclaimed his weapon.

Liz was somewhat stunned by the harshness of Will's tone, but out on the ice it was kill or be killed. Jenkins mumbled something back that was indecipherable, the knife having entered his heart and severed his aorta. Now he hung on the edge of the transition zone between this world and the next.

"Will!" Liz shouted, pulling him away from the scene.

One of the ice gorillas, like a jack-in-the-box, shot up through the ice to the amazement of all. It snarled and wasted no time in snatching up Jenkins. The animal then turned around to where Will and Liz were, but they were already boarding the snowmobile and heading away.

It charged after them, with its huge mouth wide open and roaring like some horrific creature that had just risen from the bowels of the earth. Galloping on three powerful limbs, it held Jenkins with its left arm. Biting down on the man's head it ripped it clean off, ending his battle with death. It took one look at the decapitated body and tossed it aside. The creature galloped faster toward Will and Liz after its next kill.

Will was making a beeline back toward the research center, pushing the snowmobile to the max, nearly sending Liz flying off the back as they hit a bump.

"You okay!" he shouted.

"Just drive!"

The ice gorilla was roaring like some type of rabid animal as it closed in. They could hear the creature, snarling and shrieking behind them.

Liz tried her best to put the sounds out of her mind, but it was impossible. She had this vision of the creature tipping over their snowmobile and both of them would go sliding down the throat of the animal, gobbling them whole. There would be no time to scream, no time to run, both of them would be swallowed down like appetizers.

Will's eyes spotted a crack in the ice some distance ahead. He juiced the snowmobile as it leaped up into the air, up and over the gap that had ripped through the ice shelf. The ice gorilla tried desperately to come to a stop, but the sheer mass of the animal caused it to skid. It wailed a desperate cry as it plummeted through the crevasse to its death.

Liz breathed a slight sigh of relief as she saw the ice gorilla no more. However, bringing up the rear and coming up from the right side was a pack of adult ice gorillas charging after them.

"Shit!" Will cursed.

Without warning, the entire ice shelf was again tearing and ripping new cracks over which they leaped. A new crack was now running parallel to them on the left side of the snowmobile. Liz looked at it in horror as it was cracking as fast as they were travelling.

"Will!" she shouted, as the crack all of a sudden veered sharply to the right, causing Will to swerve. The snowmobile nearly tipped over but he managed to straighten it out at the last second. The ice gorillas behind continued to charge after them, leaping and averting their own series of cracks in the ice. One after the other they successfully navigated everything on the ice shelf, pounding after the two humans.

Will and Liz were within one hundred yards of the research center when they saw Chee in the back where a helicopter hovered. Will's pulse heightened. He knew the helicopter was their only way off the ice shelf.

"Hurry!" Liz screamed.

One of the ice gorillas swiped at the back of the snowmobile, missing it by inches. Will gunned the vehicle as they jumped the fault line which was now fracturing in a confusing array of directions. The ice gorilla behind them managed to stop its body just short of the edge. The one behind it was not so lucky. It slammed directly into the first one, sending them both plunging to their deaths below.

"It's all gonna go!" Liz shouted. "This whole thing's gonna break!"

Will performed several intricate maneuvers in an attempt to outrun the cracks, but it was no use. They were completely surrounded by them. He brought the snowmobile to an abrupt halt as two unseen adult ice gorillas suddenly neared them, but they stood on the opposite side of the massive rifts. They eyed the two humans and tilted their heads slightly, in the same manner a King Cobra snake does when standing tall against prey and predator. Breathing heavily and grunting, the ice gorillas appeared confused.

"They can't get us," Will said. "The distance is too great between the cracks here."

"Yeah, and we're stuck here," Liz chimed back, terrified of the two enormous beasts that were staring at them.

The two of them remained trapped on an island of ice, surrounded by cracks that ran some twenty feet in width. They stood there, completely helpless and desperate. Liz looked over toward the research center and waved her arms. "We're over here!"

The helicopter hovered some three hundred yards away at the back of the research center. She waved her arms frantically, desperate to get the attention of the pilot.

"We've got more company!" Will yelled.

Liz turned her head. On the other side of the crack stood one of the juvenile ice gorillas, a mere runt compared to the two adults standing beside it, but still weighing in at a crushing five hundred pounds.

Chapter One Hundred-Two

The juvenile ice gorilla stood wedged in between the two adults, its red eyes glowing in stark contrast to everything around them. It was eyeing Will and Liz, several times looking in their direction and then peering down to the depths below. The juvenile began to pace back and forth, around the adults' massive pillar-like limbs.

"Where's it going?" Liz asked as the juvenile had turned its back and galloped away.

Will looked on, the scientific part of his brain taking over. "It's thinking. The juvenile is testing us. It's working out calculations. Shit!" The juvenile suddenly stopped and turned around.

Will's eyes met with its glowing red eyes as it charged toward the crevasse. Will shoved Liz behind him. "Get behind the snowmobile!"

The juvenile built up a tremendous amount of speed in no time and leaped off the edge, past the two adults, and flew through the air, landing with relative ease on the island that harbored them. Liz stood behind Will peering around his shoulder as the creature was now standing on the same platform. The only thing separating them from the hungry jaws of the juvenile ice gorilla was the snowmobile.

"Don't make eye contact," he whispered.

The juvenile's red eyes stared at Will and Liz, its jaws drooled with copious amounts of saliva. The creature took a step forward, still on all fours. They stood completely still, staring at the ice just before its feet. It stood on its back two legs for a moment and beat on its chest as Will's eyes slowly made their way up to face the creature. He couldn't resist his own advice of not making eye contact.

Fiercely agitated, the juvenile turned and charged, roaring with its mouth wide open. Will barely had enough time to reach into his back pocket. The animal hurtled effortlessly over the snowmobile and lunged for both of them. Will pushed off from Liz and rammed his switchblade deep into the juvenile's chest, the force of the collision knocking him back several feet. He instantly rose to his feet and rushed to cover Liz.

The juvenile was mortally wounded, stumbling back several feet. Letting out cries of pain, its breathing became labored and prolonged. Will and Liz looked on as it had stumbled to within several feet of the edge of the ice.

The juvenile stood up on its back two feet, mustered the strength to let out a roar as it pounded its chest and then fell backwards over the edge and down into the crevasse. The adults on the other side let out cries, watching one of their own vanish into the inky black darkness. The crevasse extended so deeply that they never heard his body hit the bottom.

The helicopter had taken off, causing the two ice gorillas to rear up on their back legs and swipe up and at the air.

"They're leaving!" Liz shouted.

The helicopter was flying exceptionally low as it approached them. Will could see the two pilots, and he waved his arms frantically at them.

"Hey!" he shouted at the top of his lungs. "Hey!"

The helicopter hovered incredibly close to them, and they saw the sight of all sights.

Liz was first to see it. "Oh my God!"

From the ice they could clearly see Chee in the cockpit. He shot the pilot point blank in the head, the man's body slumping over the controls as the helicopter dipped and lost altitude. The co-pilot grabbed the controls quickly and restored it to a comfortable height as Chee hovered behind him, gun still pointing at him, before finally returning to the back.

Will and Liz realized the possibility of being stranded on the ice shelf was real but they continued to wave their arms.

The two ice gorillas lost interest in them as they galloped after the helicopter. The first ice gorilla raced ahead of the chopper. It came to a stop, resting on all fours with its back completely exposed. The second ice gorilla charged onward, and in a moment that seemed far-fetched, it catapulted itself off the back of the first ice gorilla and launched itself high into the air.

The ice gorilla grabbed the back of the helicopter's rail, holding on to it for a brief moment. Its sheer weight caused the chopper to lose altitude before the ice gorilla came plummeting back to earth.

To Will's amazement, the ice gorilla's attempt to grab the helicopter had knocked Chee off balance and sent him flying out the open hatch door. Chee managed to grab hold of the rope ladder that also was thrust out of the chopper. Chee dangled some thirty-five feet above the ice, as the ice gorillas viciously made swipes at him, trying to bring his body to the ice. Chee was holding on for dear life.

Chapter One Hundred-Three

Saliva poured out of the ice gorilla's mouths, and driven by the primal urge to kill, they relentlessly grasped for Chee's feet, swaying back and forth like pieces of meat. Will's eyes widened as Chee was finally ripped from the rope ladder when one of the ice gorillas managed to grab hold of his feet. He fell to the ice. His body lay motionless.

"Is he dead?" Liz whispered, hardly able to bring herself to watch the situation.

He was now at the feet of the ice gorillas, peering down at him. They quickly turned their attention back toward the helicopter as it banked hard right and was heading back to them.

"Here it comes!" Will said, feeling a new surge of adrenaline course through his body, breathing new life into him.

The ice beneath him began to crack, and Liz began drifting away from him.

"Quick, grab me!" he yelled with his outstretched hand.

She grabbed his hand as he jerked with all his might and pulled her over the crack that had now formed. The area where she had been standing crumbled like a building being demolished and fell to the dark depths below. They now stood on an area of ice barely large enough to support them. The chopper hovered as the rope dropped toward them. Will pushed Liz forward, sensing their sliver of ice was seconds away from collapsing.

She grabbed hold of the ladder and began to climb as it swayed back and forth. Will did his best to steady the bottom of the rope for her. Suddenly, the entire ice field gave way, millions of tons of ice turning to rubble as everything fell away from his feet into the waters below. Firm ice was instantly reduced to falling pieces.

Will's body fell downward, completely caught off guard by the implosion. His hand reached up as he fell, managing to grab hold of the bottom rung of the ladder as the entire plateau of ice collapsed. He hung, suspended, dangling over what now resembled a massive sinkhole.

Liz called out. "Will!"

She began climbing down the rungs toward him.

"Go back!" he shouted. "Go back!"

The wind was now whipping them both back and forth. The pilot did his best to steady the chopper, but the winds were strong, threatening to send them all plummeting down the massive hole where once firm ice stood.

Liz reached down with her hand as Will clung to the ladder with his right hand, his body hovering over the frigid water, his tomb for the rest of time if his strength gave out. She tried but he was too heavy and the lift was far too awkward to pull him up. He struggled to retain his grip but gravity was so, so strong.

Come on Will. Don't give up now, he thought. *You can do it. Just lift yourself up with one arm.*

His mind flashed back to his elementary school gym class when he wasn't able to successfully climb the agility rope. He couldn't pull himself up with both arms then, but was determined to do it now.

The pain in his right hand came shooting through his body, making the urge to let go all the more tempting. He held on though, fighting for his life as the wind gusted. His thumb and forefinger slid off, and he was now supporting his weight fully with his remaining three fingers.

His eyes locked with Liz's for a brief moment and time seemed to stand still as her terrified eyes looked into his.

"Come on, Will, you have so much more to do in life. Now pull yourself up!"

Like a ton of bricks, Will Freeman felt a sense of hope like he had never experienced before in his entire lifetime, a hope for the future, a sense of belonging, and the overwhelming belief that he would be okay. That was all he needed, as he slowly pulled himself up hanging by three fingers, performing the ultimate one-handed pull-up. When his body was up high enough, he grabbed hold of the rope with his left hand.

Quickly he looked up at Liz. "Go!"

She made her way up the rope with agility and skill. He was slow to follow, falling chest first, at long last, onto the floor of the helicopter, hoisting himself through the door. As the helicopter soared away, both of them gazed down at the enormous opening in the ice where they once had been stranded.

"You folks okay?" the pilot shouted back.

Will sat directly opposite Liz. He smiled at her. "You know, I think we're going to be okay. Now can you please take us home?"

"Roger that," the pilot said.

Chapter One Hundred-Four

Will strode confidently across the stage of the dimly lit auditorium that was jam-packed with some five hundred people. He now sported a beard that gave him a distinguished appearance. The pain of Zac's disappearance one year ago still hung heavy in his heart as he approached the podium.

Behind the podium stood a giant cardboard banner that read, New York Times' Best Selling Author Dr. William Freeman.

"Thank you, everyone," Will said, adjusting the microphone while receiving a standing ovation. "Thank you, but let me earn the applause. Let me earn it."

The applause kept going for several more moments before settling down. Will took a sip of water before he began. "Once again, thank you to everyone for coming. Without you this night wouldn't be possible."

"No. Thank you, Dr. Freeman," someone shouted from the far corner of the auditorium, "Thank you for showing us that there are still mysteries in this world." The man's praise drew a further applause from the crowd. Will smiled and waited once more for the cheering and clapping to die down.

"We gather here tonight for a rather interesting topic," Will said. "Something that defies logic, defies all that is rational in the world, and yet shows us that we truly don't know our planet Earth as well as we think we do."

He paused, allowing his words to fully soak in. "Drop anyone into one of the many rainforests of the world, and if they are brave enough to pick up one of the many insect inhabitants, there is a very good chance that it will be brand new to science, something that has never been discovered. This is why our world has so many mysteries yet to reveal and why I am somewhat opposed to space travel."

This statement drew some buzzing amongst the crowd, as whispers back and forth could be heard.

"How can we travel into the farthest reaches of the solar system, spend gobs of money, when we don't even know our own planet? The oceans of the world are a mystery unto themselves. The deserts, jungles, rainforests, treetop canopies, and just about every other ecosystem remain shrouded in mystery. Just when we think we know this planet, how it functions, reacts to certain global climatic changes, and the creatures that inhabit it, it shows us something we never would have expected."

The audience was intrigued by the blow-up of the cover behind Will that read, "The Ice Gorilla." The glaring red eyes against the white backdrop of the ice shelf projected a fierce contrast.

Will picked up the microphone and began to stride across the stage. "This world is an amazing place, and that is why it's so important that we preserve what's left of it, both flora and fauna."

This drew a large applause from the audience, and as Will waited for the crowd to quiet down once again, he couldn't help but notice

Liz who was standing to the far left, backstage. She gave him a thumbs up. He smiled at her. He spoke for a few moments longer and then he drew the microphone slowly to his mouth as the cheers died down. "I leave you all with this question, the ice gorilla, fact or fiction?"

Not a soul stayed seated as everyone in attendance rose to their feet with a thunderous applause.

Dean Adams walked across the stage. "Ladies and gentlemen, Dr. Will Freeman."

Dean Adams shook Will's hand, and they both paused for several photographs in the middle of the stage.

"Will, that was brilliant. Thank you for coming tonight."

He smiled and shook his head. "Thanks for having me."

Dean Adams posed with him for one more photo before stepping aside.

Liz kissed Will on the cheek, sneaking up on him.

"You were great tonight," she said. "Zac would have been so proud of you."

He returned the smile.

Will, Liz, and Dean Adams watched as the last few members of the audience filed out the doors.

From the rear left corner of the dim auditorium, a voice spoke, "I do believe," causing Liz and Dean Adam's heads to turn in that direction.

"It is fact, Mr. Freeman."

Will's eyes went wide as Chancellor Stephen Chee stepped out into the bright auditorium light.

"But it can't be," Will muttered. "It can't be."

Will stepped toward the edge of the stage, still disbelieving what he was seeing. "You fell. You fell to your death."

His mind began replaying the instant Chee was ripped from the ladder of the helicopter by the ice gorillas. Hoping to find a solid answer as to what happened, what greeted him was a jumbled array of moments, sights, colors, and images. He turned around to Liz who was in disbelief herself.

Chee stood in the light of the auditorium basking in all his glory, with a smile from ear to ear.

Chapter One Hundred-Five

The ice vehicle slowly but surely chugged its way across the white landscape of the Canadian Arctic. The vehicle bore the name Chee Enterprises on both sides. Fog poured in from all directions as the driver nervously continued on, never having found himself in such dire conditions before.

"This is fucking crazy," he muttered, not able to see a thing.

The driver was in his early twenties, having decided to forego his last semester of college in order to take the expedition gig. His life going nowhere and he could use some money.

Visibility was minimal, not much past the windshield. Out of the corner of his left eye, he could have sworn that he saw red, two red dots glitter out in the fog bank.

The engine mysteriously came to a halt. The driver frantically tried to get it to start, his hands shaking like a leaf.

"Don't do this to me now. Come on!"

A streak of red quickly flashed in and out of view. He sat there frozen, peering out the windshield as red dots emerged from every-where .

Rolling his driver's side window up as quickly as he could, the glowing red eyes bore down upon the helpless student and the stalled ice vehicle.

The Ice Gorilla

About the Authors

Michael Esola

Michael currently serves as the Founder of the Prehistoric Channel, an online community dedicated to empowering and inspiring individuals to learn about the Earth's prehistoric past. He divides his time between writing and supporting the growth of the Prehistoric Channel to a worldwide community. Michael earned his Master of Arts Degree from the University of San Francisco. He has co-authored, "You Have A College Degree, Now What?" and "Mousecatraz: The Disney College Program." To learn more about Michael please visit www.MikeEsola.com.

Wesley Jones

Wesley has worked for organizations such as: The Walt Disney Company, Six Flags Inc., Target Corporation, and Michael Flatley's Lord of the Dance. Wesley is a certified professional in human resources (PHR) and has earned his Master of Science and Master of Arts Degree from the University of San Francisco. He has co-authored, "You Have A College Degree, Now What?" and "Mousecatraz: The Disney College Program." He currently serves as an Adjunct Professor at the University of Phoenix in the Hospitality/Tourism and Business Management departments.